PRAISE FOR BRIANNA R. SHRUM

Kissing Ezra Holtz (and Other Things I Did for Science)

"Realistic and will resonate with many teens. Give this to readers who love witty, humorous love stories mixed with STEM." —*Booklist*

"Predictable hate-becomes-love romance is given new life by an inclusive cast. . . . Worth picking up." —*Kirkus Reviews*

The Art of French Kissing

"Fun, flirty, foodie, and filled with way more heat than your average kitchen, *The Art of French Kissing* has all the ingredients for a perfect summer romance!" —Dahlia Adler, author of *Behind the Scenes*

"I ate up this hate-to-love-and-back-again romance! If you love *Top Chef* but wish more of the show was focused on the romance and rivalries behind the scenes, you'll eagerly devour *The Art of French Kissing*. Like the best sweet and savory pastries, Carter and Reid deliver both sugar and spice." —Amy Spalding, author of *The Summer of Jordi Perez (and the Best Burger in Los Angeles)*

"This meet-cute romance stands out thanks to the nuanced characters and subtle treatment of bigger issues such as race, gender, and money (Carter's family flirts with poverty). . . . A thoughtful and delicious romance." —*Kirkus Reviews*

How to Make Out

"An addictive mix of heart, humor, and hot. *How to Make Out* is the perfect lesson in how to fall in love with YA romance." —Gina Ciocca, author of *Last Year's Mistake*

"How to write a seriously addictive book? Mission accomplished. Smart, hilarious, and un-put-down-able, *How to Make Out* will capture readers' hearts." —Laurie Elizabeth Flynn, author of *Firsts*

"Full of humor, heart, and some serious chemistry, *How to Make Out* is a fun and romantic read with dynamic characters I won't soon forget." —Chantele Sedgwick, author of *Love, Lucas*

"This is a story with an obvious lesson to it, but the lesson is delivered in an entertaining manner and will be an easy sell to teen girls." —*VOYA Magazine*

"This laugh-out-loud coming-of-age novel engages readers immediately and never lets go . . ." —*School Library Journal*

THE
LIAR'S GUIDE
TO THE NIGHT SKY

ALSO BY BRIANNA R. SHRUM

Never, Never
How to Make Out
The Art of French Kissing
Kissing Ezra Holtz (and Other Things I Did for Science)

THE LIAR'S GUIDE TO THE NIGHT SKY

BRIANNA R. SHRUM

Sky Pony Press
New York

Sky Pony Press books may be purchased in bulk at special discounts for sales promotion, corporate gifts, fund-raising, or educational purposes. Special editions can also be created to specifications. For details, contact the Special Sales Department, Sky Pony Press, 307 West 36th Street, 11th Floor, New York, NY 10018 or info@skyhorsepublishing.com.

Sky Pony® is a registered trademark of Skyhorse Publishing, Inc.®, a Delaware corporation.

Visit our website at www.skyponypress.com.

10 9 8 7 6 5 4 3 2 1

Library of Congress Cataloging-in-Publication Data is available on file.

Cover design by Daniel Brount
Cover photo credit: Getty Images

Print ISBN: 978-1-5107-5780-6
Ebook ISBN: 978-1-5107-5781-3

Printed in the United States of America

For my cousins.

We all know the place to be has *always* been
wherever the cousins are hanging out.

IT'S NOT THE COLD of everything around us that gets to me in these last five minutes—it's the heat building in me.

The way my mind races hot and fast, knowing there's no way out of this cave.

The warmth that spreads through my body against the furious wind outside, the snowy walls of this makeshift den—warmth that feels a whole lot like those last hazy seconds before sleep.

The smoke and red in Jonah Ramirez's eyes when he grabs my jaw and says through clenched teeth, "Don't. Hallie Jacob, if you give up on me now, if you leave me alone up here, I will *never fucking forgive you.*"

I blink.

Slow.

Breathe.

One Mississippi.

Snow and wind beating against the trees, the ground, everything, everything.

Two Mississippi.

Lightning, flash against a tree, snap and crackle and the clean stench of burning wood. They call it thundersnow, not that that matters now.

1

Three.

Three.

I breathe the cold into my lungs.

It all feels like ice. But touch it long enough, and ice starts to feel like fire.

I brush my hand over Jonah's knuckles on my jaw.

The world lights up like a flare.

CHAPTER ONE

IT ISN'T THAT I don't want to be here, as much as it is that if the devil were to show up at these hipster-ass crossroads in horn-rimmed glasses and a waxed moustache and happen to offer me transport out in exchange for my soul, I'd take it.

I don't hate Colorado, I don't hate ski slopes, I don't even hate the sharp-toothed bite of the cold in my calves, the numb in my toes. I almost like the way it hurts when I sit by the fire in the lodge and ice-pick feeling returns to the frozen items I used to call fingers. It prickles, it hurts, but it makes me feel like life is returning to pieces of me. So no, I don't really hate any of it.

It's just that, god, I *loved* Massachusetts. I hate that I even think it past tense, like *Oh, right! Massachusetts died.* I don't "lov<u>ed</u>" it. I do still *love* it. If I close my eyes, I can still smell the bright crisp fog off the Connecticut River, clinging to my clothes when I strayed a little too close to the water.

I shut them tight, but not so tight that it doesn't dissipate in an instant.

Here, outside this ski lodge, it smells like weed. Like skunk rot and smoke.

And well. You know what they say.

Where there's smoke? There's Jonah.

I can hear him laughing over all the rest of them—who knows how many of my cousins and their significant others and their who-knows-whoevers. I want to go find them.

I want to distract myself with what they're smoking. I want to know what it is Jonah's laughing about so loud, but I'm not really allowed. I don't know how intensely your parents can really ground you two months out from eighteen, but if I'm hanging out alone in the dark anywhere Jonah Ramirez is, and I come back into the suite smelling like weed, I'll find out.

My parents are kind of assholes about my dad's brother's kids—Jolie and Jaxon (maddening, the same-letter-first-name thing. Thank god they stopped at two). Everyone knows it's more about the super Family Drama on the CW history between my dad and my uncle than it is about Jolie and Jaxon. But my cousins have given my parents enough reasons, I guess, for them to feel okay about being total jerks. Jolie is cool but a little artsy, a little follow-your-heart, a little vegan for their tastes. And Jaxon, well. Jaxon is a fucking disaster.

I like him because he always shows up to family gatherings in clothes that are super politically inflammatory and his hair is always cut weird and different and he always finds me and talks to me like he cares what I think about anything. He drops f-bombs too loud and has too many tattoos, and the same shit I think is great about Jaxon Jacob is the same shit my parents can't stand about him.

Side note: Dad and Uncle Reuben pretend they hate each other because of four decades of bad blood that everyone knows about but no one's allowed to mention. But, I don't know. If I'm putting money on it, I'd say it's gotta be *this* bullshit: Jaxon and Jolie Jacob. Jaxon. And Jolie. Jacob. How much can you *really* trust people who do this to their children on purpose?

It's complicated, I guess. Always eggshells when we're together because my parents make a big show out of being Disapproving™ of Uncle Reuben and, by extension, his wife and their offspring. And Uncle Reuben plays back, and I have to pretend I'm not on my cousins' side. But they don't outright *ban* me from hanging out with them. There's a line, I guess.

They just ... say uppity things the second we leave, acting like we escaped something when we head back to Massachusetts after a weekend (because that's all they can handle), getting to big family events as late as possible and leaving as early as semi-politeness allows. They don't like to hear me talk much about what we do when we're together either; mostly we see them or they see us and then everyone leaves and we pretend, as a family, that it never happened.

Well. Guess that's all in the past now.

Anyway.

Jaxon and Jolie, and my Favorite Cousin relationship with them, my parents can *pretend* to ignore.

Jonah, they can't.

Jonah has been Jaxon's best friend since middle school so they've been attached at the hip since we were all kids. It's almost like he's one of them—requisite J name and all.

My parents have made it extremely clear that, in their minds, all of Jaxon's *activities* are at least 75 percent Jonah's fault, and that's totally not true if you ask me, but they never do.

So.

Here I am.

On this cool family-bonding ski trip, listening to my parents and my dad's five siblings laughing adultily over their chardonnay or whatever in the common room in front of the fireplace. And I'm just sitting here in the stairwell.

Alone.

Bonding as *hell*.

I scrape my teeth over my lip and lean my head against the wall; it's kind of unsettlingly wet, but I'm assuming that's because of the, you know, snow everywhere. People tromp into a ski lodge with their boots all iced over and their coats covered in powder, stuff gets a little wet. It's not a big deal.

None of this is a big deal.

Moving away from Massachusetts my *senior year* isn't a big deal, and neither is navigating this big family weekend that I'm already kind of tired of, and neither is the reason we had to move here in the first place. My zayde basically dying—one foot in the grave at the very least—isn't ... it isn't a big ...

I'm sniffling now, in this dark hallway in a very fancy ski lodge all alone, which is totally pathetic.

I feel even more pathetic when the door opens and my cousin Tzipporah's tall, sleekly braided, absurdly gorgeous girlfriend about trips over me.

"Oh my god." She catches herself on the cement corner of the wall and I just cough.

"Sorry," I say.

"For what? Existing?"

I raise an eyebrow.

"I should have been watching where I was going. Peripheral isn't as good from this height." She winks and yeah, it's abundantly clear why Tzipporah is into her. In addition to the old Tall Dark and Handsome—well, not handsome. Tall, Dark, and Stunning—combo, she's super funny, laid back, not just *cool*. Good lord, am I sweating?

"Nah," I say. I smile; she has a face you want to smile at. "I shouldn't have been sitting . . . you know. On the floor."

She tilts her head and says, "Hallie—is that right?"

"Yeah. I totally forgot your name; I'm so sorr—"

"Samantha. Everyone forgets it. Well, I don't know why I said that; it's Sam. I like Sam. *Samantha* just has like, so much straight girl energy to it."

I smirk and snort and she sinks down beside me. Usually I'm not super into small talk, but Sam is genuine. This will at least be medium talk, and medium talk I can do.

Sam looks, like *really* looks, at me and sees the pink in my eyes, I guess, because her voice softens. "I'm sorry," she says. "About your grandpa."

I purse my lips and pull them up to the side a little, like that's going to help me not just start crying again.

"I'm fine." The lie rolls off my tongue easier than the

truth would. It's easy to tell little untruths like that when the alternative makes people uncomfortable. It's always been easy.

Well. It would be easy if my voice weren't so thick from all the weeping.

I say, in a forced bout of honesty, "We're not even super close. I don't know why I'm being like this."

Sam shrugs and says, "Grief is weird, man."

And I say, "Yeah." Then I apologize because she shouldn't have to deal with this from a stranger. Tzipporah is pretty cool, and Sam is REALLY cool, and I suddenly feel so extremely, dictionary-defined *uncool* sitting here shortly next to her, feeling sorry for myself.

"Come outside. That's where the cousins are, and you know the only place to hang out at a family thing is where the cousins are."

I laugh, because this is pretty comfortable. And I almost just say *Screw it* and go with her. But I hesitate—which, honestly, I spend a fair amount of my time doing. The lines have been pretty clearly drawn by my parents. And in lines, I am comfortable. I glance out the window one last time, and I have to make myself say, "I can't."

"Why not?"

"Just—Jonah. Jonah Ramirez? Is out there? And everyone's smoking. My parents will kill me."

"Jonah Ramirez?" Sam starts to wrinkle her nose, then remembers and rolls her eyes. "Right. Right, your parents and all their . . ." She wiggles her fingers.

I shrug. "My parents." I mimic the hand gesture. "And all their."

She sighs and looks back out the window into the black, snow falling in fat flakes. "Listen," she says, "if I just tell everyone to lay off the weed, will you—"

"NO," I say frantically. "I mean. Just. No. No, don't worry about it."

Christ, what a nightmare if she actually *had* done that. If she'd actually made everyone stop smoking on my account. I would never recover from that hit to my reputation; I'm sure it's damaged enough being the good girl rich kid with the asshole parents from ~Massachusetts~.

"I'm pretty wiped anyway, so I might just head to bed."

"You sure?" she says.

"Yeah. Yeah, I'm fine."

"Okay," she says. "If you're sure," and she's so real that it almost makes me mad. Like, how dare someone that gorgeous be perfectly kind, too?

She slides up off the floor and practically glides when she leaves, tossing this effortless "See you tomorrow?" over her shoulder.

I feel crumpled.

I feel, well, kind of weirdly comforted.

I feel . . . young. I'm seventeen, just this side of being an adult, and Tzipporah and Sam are just juniors in college, not *that* much older than me but, god, I feel like such a kid.

I wouldn't feel this way if I could hang with Jolie, maybe, pull her away from the weed and throw back a pint of ice cream and talk too loud and too detailed about each other's lives, like it hasn't been a year since we've seen each other.

But I have the whole weekend. And they have their Jonah and their weed.

I'm sleepy anyway, I guess. I sigh, pull myself off the floor and up the stairs.

And what do you know? I actually do go to bed.

In the morning, it seems everyone is skiing.

Communing with nature and shit.

I can see why—mountain peaks that stab into the sky, covered in snowfall like glitter. Fat, bright trees dusted with powder. Clouds like spun sugar covering the ground in white.

You know.

Snow.

It smells like snow.

It looks like . . . snow.

It feels like.

Snow.

Colorado is A+, 11/10 if you want breathtaking white, white views that *sound.*

Like snow.

I try to wriggle out of skiing, because I am not built for the gorgeous, breathtaking commune-y cold; I am built for hikes in the spring, summer, and fall and reading by the fire at the first bite of frost. But despite all the rules that kept me from family last night, Dad informed me this morning, like he does every year, that family was the whole point of this trip and yes, I would in fact be skiing once again. So today, spending time bonding over frostbite with family was what I was going to do.

Jolie is the first one to see me all dolled up in my skiing gear when I head outside, and *that* I am extremely stoked about. You're not supposed to have favorite siblings, so I've heard, but I'm pretty sure favorite cousins are totally permitted, and we are each other's favorite.

I'm full-on the kid from *A Christmas Story*. Skiing gear is pricey as shit. We have money but realized I'd grown out of the good gear like right when we decided we were moving and Dad was switching jobs, so ski swap it was, and here I am.

Lucky for me, Jaxon and Jolie don't have money, so they're not out here looking like L. L. Bean models either; we're all marshmallows with pink noses. Jolie's suit is bright purple, which seems right, and Jaxon's is . . . Jaxon's is hot pink. Which . . . you know what, *also* seems right.

Jolie sees me and her eyes brighten, and she waves, a beautifully ridiculous silhouette.

Jaxon tromps right up to me in all that highlighter pink, liner dark around his gray eyes. All of the pizzazz here really makes his usually suntanned skin look weirdly pale. Hot pink doesn't do great things to winter coloring; someone ought to tell him.

Jaxon says, through the huge, toothy grin on his face, "Hey there, little cuz."

"I'm not that much littler than you." I fake glare at him, hands on my hips—or where I think my hips probably are under this giant mess of water-resistant fabric.

Jolie bumps me in the side and I almost fall over. "Missed you last night."

"I was tired," I say.

"Mmhmm," she says.

I frown, amazed I *can* in this cold. I'm surprised my face muscles aren't all frozen together. "What's that supposed to mean?"

"It means," I hear from behind me, along with the crunch, crunch, crunch of booted feet through the snow, "that we all know your parents are scared shitless of me."

I feel it on my neck when he talks. I don't move.

I just glance to the side, where Jonah Ramirez now stands an inch from my shoulder, and breathe out, "Oh, is that right?"

"That's right." He smiles and clenches a honey straw between his teeth.

Jonah is like the rest of us—in absurdly puffy ski gear he probably got off Craigslist. His is black like mine, simple. And he doesn't ... well, he kind of *does* look stupid, but he doesn't look like he even notices, which changes everything.

I guess I never really mentioned that while Past Jonah used to be this annoying gangly walking smirk, Recent Past Jonah had turned into something tolerable, and Current Jonah is just ... just a straight up *problem*. I don't know how to talk to him like a normal person, because I have no freaking idea where I'm supposed to look.

His eyes are so dark they practically glitter, and he's got this intensely perfect nut-brown skin, dark freckles dusting his cheeks and nose. Hard jawline, cheekbones, sharp smile, the works. And dimples—the *audacity* of dimples on a guy like that.

And he doesn't ski, he snowboards. Of course he *snowboards*. I'm a little nervous about his board's structural integrity, truth be told; it's scratched to hell.

Of course it is. Of course even his snowboard rides the ragged edge of safety.

"Well," I say, "I'm not my parents."

His eyebrow arches and he takes that straw out of his mouth, which I bet right now would taste like honey.

Jesus Christ, Hal; what is your problem?

He's off-limits.

And even if my parents are being pretty unfair about him, blaming Jaxon's autonomous (and not *all that* scandalous) life choices on him, there's nothing drawing me there except the air about him. The one that says he's a little dangerous.

And *Oh, he just seems so DaNgErOuS* is not exactly the opening line to an epic love story, is it?

Well.

Okay.

The danger, and the dimples.

Jolie coughs, and Jonah scrapes his teeth over his lip and kind of laughs. It's a little throaty, a tic raspy, and I assume it's the dry cold.

I hope it's the dry cold.

And Jaxon says to his *super dangerous* best friend, "Come on, Ramirez. Keep me warm on the ski lift."

"Why, Jaxon," Jonah says, pressing his hand to his chest, "that's so forward."

Then he smacks Jaxon on the back and they head to the line.

"You ready for this?" I say to Jolie.

"Oh god," she says. "If I could just . . . just stay in and read a book."

I fake a sob and we link arms, ready to brave the mountain together.

CHAPTER TWO

DAD SIDE-EYES ME THE second I make it back into the ski lodge.

"What?" I say when Jolie shoots me this knowing Uncle-Uri-Am-I-Right kind of smile and heads upstairs to change out of her soaked clothes. I'd kind of like to be doing that right now; it turns out, when you haven't skied in forever, what happens when you jump back on those long, skinny death traps is you spend a lot of time rolling down the mountain.

The number of times Jaxon and Jonah passed us, laughing their asses off (and that we recovered, only to find both of them absolutely eating it thirty yards ahead), was truly astounding. I can't even begin to imagine what every single spot on my body is going to feel like in the morning, but I can tell you this: all my skin is going to be purple.

I would like a shower, and then I would like a hot tub.

And then I would like a dang *book*.

But Dad says, "Did you have fun up there?"

He's almost formal when he speaks. Well, not formal,

not exactly, not like he's giving a speech to the board or something, just . . . refined. Mom's not quite so noticeably that way, but . . . still. She's still so—so *polished*. It makes me feel like I should refine myself a little, and usually I do, so I can feel like I'm a Jacob in their presence.

Which I almost never do.

The limited times I'm with Jaxon, with Jolie, with their cool, weird hippie parents, then—then I feel like I was born with the right blood in my veins. I feel like *they* wouldn't exactly say that; they can't feel me wishing every second I'm with them that I could make those bold, impossible choices like Jaxon, or give you a detailed theory on the nature of G-d in one breath and pick out the perfect cruelty-free eyeliner with the capability of creating the most flawless wings in the other like Jolie. They can't feel me *wanting*. If they could, they'd—I think they'd agree.

But I'm not with them, I'm with my dad. Dad speaks to me, and I stand a little taller, wipe my snow-coated hair out of my eyes. "Yes," I say. Not *yeah. Yes.*

"Did you spend the whole day with—Jolie?"

I shrug. "Most of it. Hung around a little with Sam and Tzipporah, too."

Dad glances behind me at the stairs, where Jolie is disappearing. He takes time before he speaks, measures his words. And says, "Well."

He lets it hang.

Mom joins him and when I thought, earlier, about L. L. Bean models, this is what I meant. They don't even look like they've been skiing today—Mom with her impossibly immaculate bottled blonde hair and Dad, not a speck of powder on his sleek bajillion-dollar ski outfit. The only real signal is the poles.

"Well," he finally continues, "I'm glad you girls had fun."

I blink. "Yeah?" I correct myself. "I mean, yes? You are?"

"Yes," he says, adjusting his jacket on his chest. "This weekend is about family; I told you that."

"Well . . . I know that. It's just that usually . . . I just mean with, you know. With Jaxon and Jolie, you're kind of . . ."

Dad purses his lips and Mom shifts her weight.

She says, "You know we'd never begrudge you time with your cousins."

"And Jolie's actually your age. Better that you spend time with her than all the . . . the college millennials on this trip."

I cough. "Dad, people in college aren't millennials. We're all Gen Z."

He harrumphs in the way that old people do and Mom pushes his shoulder and says, "Really, Uri. You're embarrassing the rest of us. Being so old."

I snicker and my dad says, "You're older than I am!"

She shrugs. "But I'm not embarrassing the rest of us, am I?"

Dad narrows his eyes but laughs, and I swear Mom is the only person who can make him do that. The *only* one; it's like a superpower. One I kind of wish I had.

I don't know, though, I guess it kind of makes their thing special. And that's nice to watch. It's comforting, it's secure.

"Go," says my dad. "Hang out with your cousins."

Hearing him say *hang out* is so bizarre that I expect him to follow it with *as the kids say*.

"Okay," I say. "Yeah—yes, okay, I will."

"We'll meet up for dinner at the Blue Moose in a half hour."

Ah, there it is. How much trouble can we really get into in thirty minutes?

I follow Jolie up the stairs to find out.

She told me she'd be in Sam and Tzipporah's room and the door's already open, like all the college kids here say everyone leaves the dorms. Kind of cool. So I just push my way in and I am greeted by a chorus of feminine "Hallieeeeee"s.

I smile and curtsy.

"Hallie," says one of my cousins—one of the high school–aged ones. Lydia is a freshman and everybody kind of wants to protect her; she's just that kind of person. She grabs my biceps and pulls me in the room, then shuts the door conspiratorially. "We've been laying a plan."

Lydia waggles her eyebrows. "The cousins are sneaking out tomorrow afternoon."

My face never hides surprise (or anything) particularly well, so I assume this is why practically everyone in the room collapses into laughter.

"Seriously?" I say, looking back at the most serious, oldest person in the room (Tzipporah) for confirmation.

Tzipporah, who I can usually trust to be a rule-follower (like yours truly) smiles slow and sly, berry-colored lips going from studious to mischievous. "You up for it?"

I scoff like, *Duh. Wouldn't miss it. Psshhh, of course I am. Ha ha. This seems fine.*

"She's not up for it," says Jolie, and I shoot a look at her.

"You traitor," I say.

"Come on, look at you. You're about to pass out."

"I am *not* about to pass out. I'm fine."

Jolie stares at me, clearly nonplussed and cocky about her maddeningly correct reading of me.

"I'm studying to be a firefighter, Jolie; I'm not risk-averse." *Cool. Say more stuff like "risk-averse."* "If I can handle charging into a burning building, I think I can handle sneaking out. Jesus."

"Yeah," Lydia pipes in. "She's a firefighter."

I say, "Well, I'm like half a paramedic."

Lydia wrinkles her nose. "Aren't those, like, totally different?"

I scratch at my ponytail. The sudden attention of everyone on me while I explain the intricacies of my career choice is kind of a lot. I'm practically mumbling. When I say, "Kind of but like, being a paramedic or an EMT is the best way to become a firefighter. So that's . . . yeah, anyway. Anyway I'm just saying. I'm not prissy, Jolie."

Jolie looks a little shamed, a little called out, and says, "Hey, I'm sorry. I was messing with you."

"I know," I say, although I'm not totally sure it's true. Like I said, I love Jolie; she's my favorite cousin. It just sometimes feels like . . . like I've been stifled in Massachusetts. Like growing up with my parents and away from the entire rest of my family that lives in Colorado has forced me into being this totally separate person from everyone else and I hate being singled out. Because I don't . . . I don't want to be That Person. I just want to be a Jacob.

"So," I say, mustering a confidence I don't really feel.

Really amping myself for some *rule-breaking, hell yeah, fun,*
THAT'S HOW WE HAVE FUN. JUST. SHATTERING SOME
RULES. THEY WON'T KNOW WHAT HIT THEM. THAT IS
ME. AND THAT'S HOW THIS SOUNDS. F-U-N. "What's
the plan?"

The plan, as it turns out, is to wait until late afternoon,
when all the parents are exhausted from the back pain of
barreling down a mountain and wish to retire to their wine
and cheese. Then we send a scout (Tzipporah) to inform
them that some of the elder youths are having a cousin
night and we will be out late—dinner and exploring the little mountain town.

When we get the all-clear, we head out with coats,
snacks, and various party provisions (the over-21s understand this to mean ALCOHOL, PLEASE, and at least a few
of them understand it to mean weed, because that's apparently the only thing that makes Colorado tolerable). We
meet up in the parking lot, divide into cars, and head down
the mountain to Old Snowy Ridge.

Snowy Ridge is where we are now. It's where we've gone
for years—where all the rich folks (or way-less-than-rich
family of rich folks who don't bother to consider the toll
that might take on them for family meetups, sorry, Jaxon/
Jolie/Oliver/Jonah) come to ski. Celebs ski this place.

Old Snowy Ridge is where the slope *used* to be before
all the money showed up and the family bought a new

fancier plot of land a half hour up the road. Back when it was just something medium-priced to do back in the mountains and the slopes were a little shitty and hidden and the trees weren't as cleared as they should have been. That's how they tell it to me, anyway; I don't think anyone here remembers Old Snowy Ridge the way it was in its heyday.

They know it as the place adults sometimes go to snowshoe At Their Own Risk and the place you go to party when you don't want ski patrol and cops up your ass.

I've never been.

It seems ... a little risky, I guess, night hiking in the woods, but some of the cool advanced-at-the-time solar lights are still up there, trails snowshoed enough that it's probably not a big deal. Plus, at least a few of my cousins have snuck up there a million times.

I think I'm just nervous because I'm a baby. But hell if I'm gonna let *them* figure that out. I'm going whether or not my nerves are rattling in my body.

I pack so much shit, though.

Like.

Enough shit that it's going to weigh me down—*What if we get hungry? What if it's colder than we think it's gonna be? What if someone gets hurt and needs first aid? It would be stupid of me not to take this kit; I'm going to be a paramedic/firefighter for goodness' sake; this is not me being paranoid. No one else is going to do this; it's up to me. Maybe a blanket. Maybe—well, I can't fit two. What if? What if, what if, what if . . .*

My bag is super heavy with *what ifs*.

But dammit.

If someone needs some toothpaste or some Doublemint for some breath-based emergency, well, THEN who will be laughing?

I pack some gum.

I pull everything out to double-check.

Like a completely reasonable person, I pack it all again.

CHAPTER THREE

IT FEELS SO MUCH more dangerous, so much edgier than it is, piling into these two old vehicles with the cousins. I mean, I guess it *is* a little dangerous; Tzipporah's truck is only really built for four, three comfortably—the backseat is miniscule—and five of us are packed into it like sardines. Seems fine in the dark in the mountains in the snow.

I swallow and lean my head up against the back seat, ears smushing themselves between Jolie and Lydia. If I breathe, no one will know how nervous I am about all this. I'm not nervous! I'm cool!

Note how cool I am.

Note all the breathing.

Tzipporah has Top 40 on the radio, which seems about right because that's the most likely to universally appeal to everyone here—this is the girls' car. The boys are in Jonah's beater coupe, and there's only three of them coming tonight so they're probably a little more comfortable than we are, but also it's close quarters and the boys' car so it probably smells like BO in there. Or who knows what.

Whatever it is, it's too chilly to justify rolling the windows down, so it can't be an ideal scenario.

We wind our way down from this mountain and then up to the other, and the mountains seem so much more treacherous from here. The roads are windy and thin, nothing like they are in the Northeast. There, everything is built around cow paths. Here, transportation is carved into ancient stone. It feels too shallow, too high, like every hairpin is taking a risk, even though it's not even dark. The roads are barely icy. I see guard rails.

I lean back against the headrest as talk quiets and stare out at the mass of trees below me, and Tzipporah turns up the radio, and I ignore as best I can the snake of a road barely scraped into the mountain until we hit Old Snowy Ridge.

We fall out of the truck in a pile, everyone laughing and high on the forbidden fake danger of everything. I'm laughing, too, as my cheeks and nose pink and what feels like a billion cousins and friends bump into me from all sides.

"Ladies?" Jaxon calls, and Very Gay Sam catcalls back at him. He studiously ignores her, and we congregate.

The dark descends with the snow, way earlier than I think it will.

But what do I know? I'm reminded every year that this isn't the place that's mine, and now I'm reminded again, like always, because I don't even know when it gets dark up here.

But it's like five, and already the sunlight feels gray.

The temperature drop, even though it's only a few degrees, is breathtaking in the dry cold when we leave the truck.

I run my hands fast up and down my arms inside my coat, even though no one else is doing that. Massachusetts gets cold, but it's not like just because I lived somewhere that snows, I'm immune to it. That's not how that works.

My breath clouds on the air and Jolie bumps my shoulder. "You gonna survive the night, Yankee?"

I roll my eyes. "Please, I'm fine. At least it's not a humid cold. The humid cold—"

"Soaks into your bones."

She says it at the same time that Jaxon does; she and Jaxon are so different, but sometimes being around them is like living life in stereo.

"Dry cold is like being freeze-dried," says Jaxon.

"Yeah, yeah," I say to Jaxon and they both grin—he looks mischievous, she just looks bright-eyed. Excited. She's bouncing on her toes.

Though in fairness, that could just be the cold.

I zip my coat and pull my beanie over my ears and my backpack out of the trunk, then sling it over my shoulders.

"I guess it's kind of a humid cold," says Jolie. "It's been raining all day on this mountain."

"Mm," says Jaxon, tossing his head so his hair falls out of his eyes for a half second. "Well, it needed it. Elk getting thirsty and all that after the half-drought."

I shrug. Jaxon just isn't the kind of guy you'd expect to be the walking Division of Wildlife, and yet, here we are.

"Come on," says Jolie. "Up this way."

I say, "Okay," and follow them into the growing dark.

The stars aren't out yet or anything; it's not *nighttime*. It's just evening in the mountains, which feels like nighttime anywhere else. The clouds are spitting out these occasional fat flakes—one every few seconds so it's like they're being worked on individually, meticulously.

A few cousins are laughing up ahead as we walk the trail back to debauchery mountain.

The snow crunches beneath our feet and my big, puffy (warm as heck) coat swishes every time I move my arms.

But beyond that?

It's just . . . silent.

Nothing but the woods—the specific, cool dark of the light gray clouds in the sky and the sun looking for a place to truly retreat. The crisp smell of pine and snow (because evergreens and aspens are all that can make it in Colorado, altitude and cold and lack of oxygen considered). The sounds of absolute emptiness.

I want to stop right here, let them all move ahead and melt in it.

I don't, obviously. This is the mountains. I don't want to like . . . get attacked by a roaming pack of wolves or something.

But the *silence* in these woods. It's so different than the woods back east. There, no matter where you go, you're surrounded by life. By sound. If it's not squirrels rattling the branches, it's birds singing. It's cicadas screaming. It's bugs under your feet and life burrowing into the trees.

Here, it's truly, *truly* quiet. Here, you can just . . . be away. Even from the bugs and birds.

What a revelation.

We crunch along, further and further into the woods,

some of us lugging bags and some of us lugging logs and who knows what else, until we get to the place that Tzipporah loudly declares is The Spot.

The Spot is a really great clearing in the middle of the trees, whose boughs have largely protected it from snowfall. Not completely, there's still patches, and it's not like the snow is inches deep or something anyway, not here, not on this side of the mountain.

But there's a few rocks piled up in the memory of a campfire, and I wonder if they've made one here before (probably) or if it's been others who have used this as their spot and Tzipporah and Sam just discovered it and we're taking it as our own (also likely).

"Alright," says Tzipporah. "Men. Assemble the campfire. It is not warm out here."

"Aye, aye," says Jaxon, saluting. He flings the bag off his back and dumps the logs in the pit in a way that Jonah apparently finds dissatisfying, so he goes to take over and Jaxon pretends to be offended for like four seconds before he happily gives up and goes to sit on one of the big logs that's been set up around it. Oliver, Lydia's BFF and honestly a year too young to have fairly made the age cutoff for this outing (he's in the eighth grade), stands there looking awkward until Jonah finishes up.

I set my bag on the ground and make my way to one of the unoccupied logs, glancing up at the sky. It's still not nighttime, still this gray on the precipice of going black.

We've been hiking for like an hour, so yeah, it's gotten later.

I shiver, and it's definitely the cold; it's not because I'm nervous. Everyone knows their way around here. Everyone knows how to mountain.

I say, all cool, definitely cool, "So how do we, like, find our way back?"

Jonah says, still focusing on the log formation, "Bread crumbs." I groan and he glances back over his shoulder at me, mouth curling. "Landmarks," he says. "And little pieces of yellow ribbon marking the path."

"Ah."

"As though Tzipporah would let us just hike back here without marking trees and shit; come on. I'm surprised she didn't video the whole hike step by step."

I laugh. "Yeah, okay, fair."

Tzipporah, from somewhere just inside the trees, says, "I heard that."

I laugh harder. "Who was in charge of that?"

"Who do you think?" says Jonah. "The Eagle Scout."

"You're—an Eagle Scout?"

"Mm," he says. "That surprise you?"

"Well." I shift on the log. "Seems a little goody two-shoes for you."

He laughs, throaty and smoky, and glances at me with those dark brown eyes again, and I can feel it in the pit of my stomach. "Yeah," he says.

"So you're the guy who gets us back out of here?"

"What?" He messes with those logs, looks up at me again from his crouch. His voice is low when he says, "Don't trust me, Jacob?"

"DOWN," says Jaxon.

Jonah stands and steps away from the campfire. "Hmm?"

"Down, boy. Stop hitting on Hallie. Jesus."

"Ah, come on," he says.

My face flames, even in the cold.

"No," he says. He points a long, slender finger at Jonah and basically wags it. "Get your charming ass away from her. Hallie, stay strong. The soulful brown eyes are a trap."

"Aw, you think I'm soulful?" He grins. "How about you?" he says to me. "You think I'm soulful?"

His eyes are sparkling in the dim light, and I can't really breathe with the full force of his attention turned on me.

"That's a trick question, Hallie; don't answer it. Jonah, stay away from the high schooler and sit by me."

Jonah just raises an eyebrow at me and I say, "I don't know if *soulful*'s the word for it."

"Nah?" he says.

"No."

"What's the word for it?"

"Trying too hard."

He spits out a laugh and says, "Christ," just as Jaxon starts clapping.

Jonah plops down by him, and they start talking about who knows what and my pulse is ripping through my veins, even though Jaxon is right: this is how Jonah talks to everyone.

Thankfully, Sam comes to sit beside me and starts asking me about Massachusetts and laughs when I call a water fountain a "bubblah" in an exaggerated-for-her-benefit-I'm-not-from-Boston! accent. Night closes in a little deeper, and someone cracks open a beer, and then everyone is cracking open beers, and Rules-Following Tzipporah is surprisingly cool with everyone drinking underage.

I've never seen her like this, I guess.

But Old Snowy Ridge feels like a different world.

It's Jaxon who pulls out the weed—surprise, surprise. Every dude takes a hit, even fourteen-year-old Oliver who definitely should *not* and totally chokes on it, and on the girls' side, the only two who pass are Sam (kind of a surprise) and Lydia (definitely not a surprise) and so I take one, too.

I've smoked before. Once.

I cough a little and catch Jonah's eyes across the bonfire haze. He's smiling at me, just a little. Infuriatingly cocky. Infuriating or . . . well.

Something else that gets me a little hot.

The cousins and the friends they brought are laughing in these little groups that I want so badly to be a part of.

You serious? Uncle Bernie? Uncle BERNIE was fucking nuts in college, man. He got thrown in the can for like twelve different fights.

Absolutely not. That's bullshit.

Ask him!

Oh, I'm sure he TOLD you that, dumbass, but he's been in like three, tops.

No dude, you're wrong. I've seen his arrest record.

Bullshiiiiiittttt.

It's all fights and communism and protests all day long.

An eye-rolly jack-off motion.

Or across the aisle: *Game Of Thrones, oh how fucking original to love Game of Thrones.*

I like the Lannisters!
You just have a thing for blondes.
Yes. Yes I do.
Or right next to me:
Mmmm, never have I ever made out with a friend's ex.
Never have I ever gone with two dates to a dance.
Never have I ever started a mutiny in class.
Never have I ever started my period in the middle of gym, pan-
icked, and told the coach I'd done the splits and ripped my VAGINA
OPEN because somehow that seemed more logical and less embar-
rassing than "It's my regular, normal menstrual period and it's still
irregular, whoops, I bled through my underwear."
OH MY G-D I TRUSTED YOU. I WAS ELEVEN.

Jaxon is lying back on the pine-needled ground behind the log now, looking up at the stars that have come out, and I just watch him. He looks so peaceful. Stoned, but he's not stoned. That's just how he is: at ease.

I'm not out of it either; of course I'm not. One hit of this weed isn't enough to get me high as much as it is to relax me just a little.

Just enough to enjoy this whole night without anxiety eating me alive.

I glance at the log again, sparks from the fire dancing, crackles and pops making the nighttime come alive.

And we just get to live in it.

The freedom is . . . kind of intoxicating.

Jonah is looking at me again, corner of his mouth tipping up. He's tapping his finger on his knee, looking up at the sky for a second, looking back at me.

I mouth, *What?* And I'm smiling. I'm smiling like an

idiot. I know exactly what he's trying to do and it's exactly what he's done with a million other girls, I'm sure, and he's not going to get to me. He's absolutely not.

He shrugs, mouths, *What?* back at me.

I mouth, *You.*

He furrows his brow and presses his hand to his chest. Like he's so offended.

I narrow my eyes even though my mouth is smiling, even though I can feel his attention buzzing over my skin. I try to say soundlessly, *You know what you're doing.*

But he just shakes his head and points to his ear. *Can't hear you,* he mouths.

I exaggeratedly roll my eyes and try to say it slower.

He cuts me off in the middle of the sentence by cocking his head toward the tree line.

I bite my lip.

I shouldn't.

I just . . . definitely, absolutely should not.

I curl my fingers around my Coke bottle and he cocks an eyebrow like a question.

I glance over at Jaxon, like I need his permission or something.

I'm not going with Jonah.

I'm not stupid.

I'm *not* going with Jonah.

I'm not.

Jonah's mouth tips and there's mischief and fake inno-cence and sex written in the wry line.

I'm going with him.

CHAPTER FOUR

IF ANYONE NOTICES ME disappearing into the woods with Jonah Ramirez, I don't notice them noticing. I'm too busy thinking about how *stupid*, how *thrilling* it is that I'm doing this, to worry about anyone blood related to me and what they might think about it.

The stars are out now, and it gets darker the further we get from the fire, so they're smeared across the sky like glitter. But we don't go that far. Not like the Colorado woods are super private anyway; the place isn't exactly known for conditions that favor life. The woods aren't dense. They're a little sparse—nothing but bushes and aspens that tower over them, skinny and pale. Every one of them would be dwarfed by the trees back home.

Anyway, the point is: we're not completely cut off from society or the bonfire when we decide we've gone far enough. The point is that I can still kind of hear everyone laughing, but the sounds all bleed together like paint in water. The point is that it's dark but not rainforest-tree-covered dark. There's enough space for the moon to shine in and illuminate the planes on his gold-brown face, the shadows at his jawline. His eyes are really, really dark, I notice, and he's got that dimple when he smirks. Just the one, I realize, standing this close to him. Paying attention.

He's always looking for trouble, I think, so that dimple is always there.

"So," he says, "tell me why we've never talked."

I shrug. "We've talked."

"Not like this."

"Well, I never go to the woods."

He smiles. "We should have hung out."

"Yeah?" I say.

He says, "Yeah. You're Jaxon's favorite, you know."

I can't hide the smile at that. "Bullshit."

He's chewing on another one of those honey straws and I can't stop looking at his mouth. "Nah," he says. "Not bullshit. He loves you."

I lean against the aspen at my back and fold my arms across my chest. A knot digs into my spine, just the slightest bit. Not enough to be super uncomfortable, but enough to make me highly aware of my own skin. Not that my skin, my body, aren't things I'm already *pretty freaking aware of* right now.

"Well," I say, "maybe you should have made more of an effort. If I'm such a delight."

He says, "I mean, your parents would have had me put under house arrest, but sure, maybe."

"You afraid of my parents?" I say, and I look directly at him. Just right the frick into his eyes. What is getting into me that's making me downright bold? Downright forward? I've *seen* Jonah a million times over the years, but it's not like I know him. It's not like we're familiar.

It doesn't matter. It's just this kind of wild night in the woods that everyone's going to get in trouble for tomorrow so none of us are going to think about that.

We both know what we want.

I mean, I certainly know what *I* want, and if I know anything about Jonah Ramirez, it's that he wants what I currently want, like, all the time.

He probably *gets* what I currently want all the time.

His eyebrow arches just for a second, and that's how I know I've surprised him. A spike of warmth thrills in my veins when he takes that honey straw out of his mouth and says, "Nope."

"You sure? My dad's an ex-Marine."

He sputters. "No shit?"

"Nah," I say. "He's an actuary."

Jonah laughs and it doesn't feel like one of those false, trying to get into your pants kind of laughs. It feels genuine. I find myself smiling. Find myself relaxing into the tree trunk at my back.

"What the hell is an actuary?"

"I'm not totally clear on it; it's a math thing. And like a business money thing."

"Well then, in that case, no. I'm not afraid of your parents."

"What if I'd been telling the truth?" I say.

"I'd take my chances, I guess."

"With what?" The words about stick in my throat. But look at me, all made of willpower. I am *smooth*.

Jonah leans against a tree, a perfect mirror of me. Except he melts into the position. It takes clear, intentional effort for me to be like this, to appear relaxed, like I know what I'm doing, like I'm totally gunning for it and expecting to get it, not like I'm a string of concern, a wash of anxiety and Type A-ness all over the place in my brain. He looks like he belongs in these woods. He looks like he owns them.

He looks like he owns every room (or non-room, apparently) he enters.

He says, "Talking. With their daughter in the woods."

"Mm," I say.

"This is verboten, right? I'm going to corrupt you if you come within thirty yards?"

"I'm pretty sure that's how it works, yeah."

"Then I'll just stay over here," he says.

I try my best to look prim. "I think that's for the best. Get any closer and I'll be swearing and smoking weed within the night."

"I saw you smoking earlier," he says.

"You did? Well, fuck."

He laughs again. Smoky and hazy and *wanting something*.

My mouth turns up. This is never me. I'm never this confident, this just absolutely balls-out about things. Maybe it's the weed. Maybe it's the woods. Maybe it's just . . . the total, immense relief at finally having a good time for five minutes after the shitstorm that the last couple months have been.

A breeze makes its way through the trees, rattling the leaves in the aspens and the needles on the evergreens. I shudder, despite the big coat, because cool wind has a way of slipping under your clothes.

Jonah says, "You cold?"

I say, "Eh."

And he kicks off the tree. He approaches me—this tall, devastatingly hot silhouette—and when he comes close, I am treated to that view of his dark freckles, the spray over his nose. Jonah's Afro-Latino, and his skin is already pretty dark, but those little freckles are three shades off of black, and the contrast is incredible.

He leans over me, heels of his hand brushing my coat. Thumb just crossing over the strands of my hair. "You want my coat?" he says.

His voice is low. Like he's telling me a secret.

I do not. Want his coat.

"I'm already wearing a coat," I say.

I try to say that boldly, like I did earlier. Like I do this kind of thing all the time. Like I'm used to sneaking off with boys I'm forbidden from talking to into the woods, looking to make out or who knows what else.

That's not how it comes out.

I am hoarse. I can't just feel my voice shaking in my throat; I can *hear* it.

There's no way he doesn't.

His lips tick up for a half second, but he has the grace not to comment on it.

"I think you're cold," he says.

His hand shifts, so I can feel it when he pulls several more strands of my hair into the crook of his thumb, brushes his fingers against them.

I'm shaking just a little bit, but it's mostly the adrenaline, I think.

I say, "Freezing."

His tongue darts out over his lips and his gaze skips from my eyes to my mouth and back up. "I don't know how you guys fix that shit up in Massachusetts. But here—"

I don't know.

I don't know how they do it here.

Because he's cut off by the most haunting groaning from the woods, like the mountains themselves are being drawn and slowly quartered.

There's the sound of trees cracking. A rush of noise. And an absolute chaos rises up from the camp.

Jonah looks up, and I push away from the tree and oh my god.

Holy shit.

The mountain is coming apart.

CHAPTER FIVE

"WHAT THE FUCK?"

It's Jolie; I can make out her voice over the frantic snapping under my feet, the utter roar of the mountain, the panic in my brain.

"JESUS, JOLIE, COME ON. WE HAVE TO GO." It's Jaxon—raw panic in his voice as he jerks her away from the camp.

"Where are they? Where's Hallie? Where's—"

"We're here!" I shout it, but I don't know if they can hear me. I don't know who can see me and who's here and which direction we need to run. All I know is that the mountain is coming *down*. Oh my god. Oh my god.

Jonah has me by the wrist, hand clamped around my bones, and he's dragging me along. It probably does make me move faster. I know if I tripped, he'd just yank me back up, and my feet are flying over the ground.

I manage to hook the backpack I brought as we sprint past the bonfire.

Mud and rock and snow rush in a roar down the mountain, and I can barely think past the lizard brain

RUN RUN RUN RUN RUN RUN RUN RUN RUN in my head.

Every muscle, every cell, every bit of blood and bone is urging me to FUCKING GO.

I don't even know where we go, I don't know which turns we make. I can barely see in the dark and neither can Jonah, and I'm sure neither can my cousins. We're just behind them, and then we're surrounded by them, the smallest stampede. Our footsteps are swallowed by the growl of the mountain.

Our panic, our fear, our sudden flight of survival is nothing in the face of this. It is an impossible roaring, it is world-altering, the *sound* of it is everything.

Anyone who saw this from the ground would hear nothing but silence.

The woods cave in, being overtaken by the rush of mud and snow, and I don't know. I don't know where it stops, where it will end, if we will all be swallowed and this is it, it's the end.

I'm freezing and I'm hot all at once.

But I'm moving.

We're all moving.

Not as fast as the mountain.

We crash through the trees, we go, we go, we go.

Until the deafening rumble quiets.

Until the woods slowly, slowly still.

Until we can step out of the falsely protective cover of the trees and look down the hill and see that we are out of its path, and it's a path no longer being carved anyway.

Until we can breathe.

I'm trembling everywhere, and my throat hurts. My head hurts. None of this feels real. The adrenaline is so intense that now *that* is the loudest sound I can hear, and I can't push past it. I squeeze my eyes shut, then open them. Shut again, so hard it hurts. Then open. I exhale. It comes out in stops and starts.

Jonah's breath is ragged beside me. I can feel his whole body shaking.

He squeezes my wrist, and then his grip loosens, like he physically can't make his fingers loop.

Without him forcing me to stand, I don't.

I collapse.

I think I remain conscious.

I don't *think* I actually pass out. But if I laid money on it, I'm not sure I wouldn't come out at a loss.

No one says a damn thing for seconds, minutes.

We are all just breathing, touching our own skin to make sure we're alive. Staring into the darkness to try to puzzle out what the *fuck* just happened, to confirm that it's real.

That the earth we had just been standing on is gone.

That the mountain, like one of those crazy videos on YouTube, just came down around us.

"Head . . . head count," says someone. Tzipporah. It has to be. Who else would it be?

No one says anything for a solid minute.

"GODDAMMIT, HEAD COUNT," she says.

And Lydia starts crying.

Sam says her own name, and Lydia sobs hers, and then we all follow, person by person.

Lydia is still sniffling.

We all gather together in a huddle, and Tzipporah makes us say our names three more times before she's satisfied that we're all here.

Thank G-d.

The trees, which seemed so much smaller earlier, seem huge and dark now, suffocating. Like binding and shelter all at the same time.

"Can we . . . can we get back to the truck?" says Lydia.

Oliver says, "No way to know, man; do you even know where we are?"

"No."

"It's dark," says Jaxon. "We're all turned around; there's just . . . there's just no way we make it down tonight."

"What the hell *was* that?" says Jolie.

Sam says, "Mudslide. It's been so dry and then the rain; I'm so stupid. I can't believe I didn't think about it. I just figured *Cool. Rain. Means we can have a fire.* I didn't . . . I should have figured . . ." She starts crying and Tzipporah wraps her arms around her.

"Why doesn't someone call for help?"

There's a collective rustle as people check their phones. But no one has service. I mean, of the, like, three of us who didn't leave phones in the cars or lose them in the chaos or leave them back at the campsite.

Sam says, "DAMMIT."

"It's okay," I say. "It's going to be fine. It's one night and it's cold, but we all have our coats. We have supplies. I mean, a couple bags, right? Who's got a bag? I have one."

"Me," says Jolie.

Sam says, "I got one."

Oliver hugs Lydia in close to his side and says, clearly trying to cover up panic that cannot be covered, "No. No, no, this is bullshit. I'm not staying up here tonight. Lydia and I aren't. We can't. All we need to do is just, like, retrace our steps—"

"Retrace?" says Tzipporah. "How, exactly? There's nothing TO retrace. The mountain ate it."

"And it's dark now," Sam pipes in.

Lydia starts shaking. "We could hike around a little. Look for like a ranger station or—"

"We are not. Getting anywhere. Tonight," says Jaxon.

Lydia sniffs.

"I'm not a fan of this either," he continues, "but doing anything other than staying put right now is suicide."

It's silent for a solid thirty seconds.

That's a shockingly long time in the city.

In the woods, alone in the cold, it's an eternity.

"Okay," I say. "So we start another fire. We can do that. We take turns keeping it alive and this will be like . . . an adventure. In the morning, we find the cars and we go home. Okay?"

Jonah is looking at me. He's quiet, contemplative. Coming down from everything, probably. Then he stands and simply starts gathering wood and pine needles.

Some people feel comfortable making plans. Me, that's me. I need a plan, I need steps A through Z, and I need to lay it out.

Jonah is someone who needs to act.

A couple cousins join Jonah in the gathering, and when the plan is underway, I can breathe.

It becomes clear to me, in the silent aftermath of everything, just how cold I am. Just how dark it is. Just how much my muscles suddenly hurt.

I blow out a shaky breath. We just . . . we just survived a mudslide.

Someone—who cares who—pulls out a lighter and ignites the growing pile of kindling.

It starts small; it really is cold out, cold enough to discourage even flame.

We all move toward the fire, everyone shivering and scared and tired and freezing and just . . . just wondering.

Wondering too many things that feel dangerous to put to words.

I wind up between Jolie and Lydia. Jaxon is on Jolie's other side and he's practically hovering over her. He's protective; he's always been like that with her. I don't think I've ever seen siblings love each other so much.

She's fine.

But he'll be like this until we're out of the woods.

Literally and metaphorically.

"My ankle hurts," says Lydia. She's fourteen but suddenly she seems so much younger than so many of us. I want to protect her.

I say, "Yeah, I sliced my hand open running. And my calves are killing me."

She nods and scoots closer to me on a log a couple of the cousins rolled over here. She lays her head on my shoulder.

I can feel the worry in the camp.

It's just one night; we really will be fine. I think. I mean, I'm pretty sure. How far can we have run? We can't be *that* turned around; it's just that it's so freaking dark and we're all running on a combination of adrenaline and absolute exhaustion.

And worry, which doesn't help.

On the other side of the fire, it's about as quiet as it is here. The whole camp is thick with unease.

It's starting to soak down into my marrow, the anxiety I was able to banish with all my reassurances and plans.

I shudder.

I want to say, "It's fine, guys! Perk up! Truly, an adventure!" But I can't. It wouldn't help anyone, and I can't make myself say something I don't really believe, not when it comes down to it. Not when it comes down to the reality that we are spending the night turned all around without a tent or cell service.

I've camped, but I've never camped without anything over my head.

A coyote—a wolf? I don't know. Are there wolves in Colorado?—howls somewhere in the distance, and I actually laugh. Because hey, as it turns out, I'm fucking terrified.

Jonah's voice is the thing that cuts through the tense silence.

He says, "I ever tell you about that time my truck broke down about ten miles from here?"

Jaxon's head pops up, and he and Jonah exchange a long look. Jaxon says, "Nah. Tell us." Like he knows something.

Jonah says, "It was dead winter, a night kind of like tonight, actually. Wind howling, wolves, snow, all that shit."

"Atmospheric," says Jaxon.

Jonah flips him the bird and says, "So I'm up here scouting and I cross this creek. It's a little hop for me. Frozen over, kind of, but anyway, not solid enough I'm gonna step on it or my boot will go right through. I hear this crack and I look back, and there's this tiny little spiderweb fracture splintering out in the ice. Like someone's walking on it. Then another a few inches away."

I furrow my brow and hug my coat around me. The smallest breath of wind whispers through the sparse forest, if you could even call it that.

Jonah says, "I don't really think about it much; I just keep walking. I saw some elk sign up the way last year, so that's where I'm headed. Well, a half mile down, I realize it's not just my footsteps I'm hearing in the dirt. I'm hearing me and these little muffled steps that are moving twice as fast, at least. Small. Like a little animal maybe? Or like . . . a little kid."

"Bullshit," Sam whispers.

An owl hoots in the distance and because I'm cool and mature, I do not immediately think it's a ghost.

"Yeah, sounds like I'm losing it. But then a quarter mile down the cow path, I see something. It's a little stuffed porpoise. And it's got its stuffing ripped out. At this point,

I'm just kind of freaked out. But it's nothing compared to what I see hanging in the trees when I follow that cow path into the pines. It's a fucking menagerie. Dolls and shit, various states of disrepair. I can hear the wind whistling, hear those little footsteps behind me; it's like a kid's horror paradise in the woods. And I don't know what the *hell* to do except I know I can't turn my back on it. Not on a place like this. Suddenly I hear those little footsteps behind me and they stop."

I'm holding my breath.

We all are.

"And this tiny little voice says something I can't understand."

I lean in.

"She says—"

Suddenly Jaxon grabs Jolie by the shoulders and shakes her and says, "I HAVE COME FOR MY REVENGE," and Jolie shrieks and we all shriek and then we're laughing in relief.

Jolie says, "You asshole!"

Jaxon is losing his shit, and Jonah is laughing, too, and he says, "Which one?"

And Jolie says, "Both of you! I HATE YOU."

Then someone else starts in on a scary story, and it's like the spell is broken.

It feels . . . unreal now.

Like a story.

Like an adventure we can make it through.

At least a bunch of us feel that way, or it seems like it. Distracted by stories and the fire.

The flames are by turns too hot and too cold, warming my front until I feel like my skin is on fire while my back freezes, then doing the opposite. Smoke stings my eyes. But the pain, the discomfort, is something to focus on.

The lateness of the night sinks in, even through the fear.

Through the hot and cold.

One by one, most of us drop into sleep.

I can't.

I'm not gonna be able to sleep all night.

I can't stop hearing those wolves.

How am I going to sleep through this cold, with nothing at all to shield me from whatever's home we are invading?

As though a tent would do that.

It doesn't matter; it's the principle of it.

Eventually, Jaxon and Jonah and I are the only ones awake.

Jaxon yawns, and I say, "Go to sleep, man. I can't. I'll stay up and keep this fire stoked."

Jaxon doesn't argue with me. He just says, "It's gonna be okay, cuz."

I say, "Yeah."

Jonah meets my eyes across the fire. They are intense, determined. Assessing the reality of the situation.

The risk.

He is concerned.

So am I.

Neither of us says anything.

We don't have to.

The fire crackles between us in the dark.

CHAPTER SIX

I DON'T THINK I slept all night.

I'm missing time; I couldn't tell you every single moment that passed in the last six hours, so I must have dozed off at *some* point. But it feels like I was up forever. My eyes are burning and I'm cold, and I look like a mess, I'm sure.

On the plus side, so does everyone else. It's not like anyone slept in a king-sized hotel bed last night, but everyone else at least got a few hours of sleep.

I got *none*.

Jonah looks like a total wreck, too.

His eyes are red and there's dark circles under them and his hair is standing up all wrong.

It's charming, or it would be if I wasn't worried about being completely exhausted and cold and stranded in the freaking woods.

I lie on the hard ground for a while, like I can fall asleep with the sun on my face and the freezing earth hard under my hips. I shut my eyes.

Nothing happens.

I'm just cold.

I'm just tired.

My eyelids are straight up glued together.

I force my eyes open—it hurts—and roll from my side up to my butt so I'm sitting up. I'm committed now, I guess. I'm up.

I stand and stretch, wrists and back and neck popping audibly.

I look around the woods, willing myself to just magically see one of Tzipporah's yellow trail markers we all teased her for earlier, one of the breadcrumbs she forced us to leave so we could find our way back home.

But it . . . it all just looks like trees.

One by one, everyone in the camp wakes up, remembers where we are. Where we aren't.

Someone digs into their pack and passes around water bottles and granola bars. No one has to say that we should ration. No one goes nuts on the food or the water or anything because last night we said we were going to be fine.

But we all know that was the kind of truth you can only tell when you have no fucking clue what's real.

I eat my bar silently.

Staring into the dead fire.

Suddenly, beside me, Lydia starts sniffling. I'm almost mad, which is shitty of me, but Jesus, dude, pull it together.

We're hardly even awake.

Calm down.

I bite down on my tongue so I won't say anything, so I can be nice to my scared, small cousin—or at least not actively mean to her.

Then I see her shift and hear her suck in a sharper breath.

"You okay?" I say, even though I'm sure she's just being young and small and sensitive.

She says, "My ankle hurts."

I say, "That sucks. Still bugging you from last night?"

Big deal, honestly; I'm sure we're all sore.

"No," she says. "I mean. Yes. But no, like. It just. It *really* hurts, Hallie."

"Walk around on it," I say. "You probably just need to stretch it or something."

Lydia sucks her lip in between her teeth and moves to stand, then hisses, and her leg collapses under her.

"Shit," I say. Guilt courses through me when her face goes a shade paler. She's not being a baby; that's an *injury*.

I'm so glad she couldn't hear what I was thinking.

"It's that bad?"

"Yeah. I just—I think I sprained it or something."

"Shit," I say again. I dig in my bag for the few first aid supplies I brought in case of something like this. (Suck it, brain—acting like I was being overly cautious! We're all welcome!)

Jaxon walks by, stretching, yawning, hair a wild mess, nose pinched with the cold. He frowns. "You okay, Lydie?"

Lydia scrunches her nose and draws in a breath. She's *really* trying to hold it together.

I'm handing her some ibuprofen and taping the foot in question when I say, "She sprained her ankle."

Jaxon shoots me a wide-eyed look and says, "That's okay. It's gonna be fine."

His face says, *She's going to get eaten by a bear.*

I watch him go from person to person, then, doing an evaluation.

He circles back around to Jonah and tells him that it's just Lydia, that the rest of us are okay, and I don't know why it feels so comforting that Jonah knows what's up and doesn't freak out. I don't even know the guy, and any of the other cousins who don't know him much better than I do seem to be perfectly content with it, like checking in on Jonah's reactions is the reasonable choice here.

Maybe it's the Eagle Scout thing; maybe it's just that Jonah has that energy that says he knows what the hell he's talking about and you should believe him.

Tzipporah clears her throat and says, "Okay. What needs to happen here is this: we are going to send a small group to explore. If it starts to rain, if it starts to snow, if anything at *all* happens that jeopardizes your ability to get back here to everyone in a reasonable amount of time, you head back."

"Cool," says Jonah.

He stands and shoves his hands in his pockets, and I hear myself saying, "Why you?" when Jaxon stands with him.

He turns his gaze on me and arches an eyebrow. "Because," he says, "I've spent a fuck-ton of time up here, and so has your cousin."

I glance at Jaxon, and Jaxon's mouth quirks up. "Weed's legal, but not if you're under twenty-one."

"It's legal at Old Snowy Ridge," says Jonah.

I groan, but I'm smiling.

Half of us are, which means that it sucks, but . . . it's okay. It's still okay.

Jaxon and Jonah leave, and it immediately seems less okay. The split in the group sends insecurity scratching over my skin.

But that's not logical; they're fine. They're going to be fine. They do know this mountain, and Jonah is an Eagle Scout, for god's sake.

And we're going to be fine here; I'm practically an EMT already thanks to the vocational classes I've been loading up on, just a couple steps from becoming a paramedic, and Sam is pre-med. If there is such thing as an ideal group to be stranded in the woods, it's ... well, okay. Let's be real. It's not us. We're a bunch of freezing cold kids who are not Jason Momoa or Bear Grylls or anyone who can live the winter in a cave they've burrowed in themselves.

Jolie runs her hand through her hair and sits beside me on a decently dry patch of pine needles. She says, "Tell me about Boston."

I stare at her. The silence thickens into something I can almost touch, like I'm almost mad. Like how dare she ask me something stupid and inconsequential and kind of painful when we are trapped in the woods?

But ... but of course she's doing it on purpose.

Of course she knows me, and she knows this is crashing through the order in my world and I'm a half a second away from snapping.

I take a breath.

"It wasn't Boston," I say. "But I can tell you about Massachusetts."

"Okay," she says. Her shoulders drop and her mouth relaxes into a smile. And maybe this is as much for her as it is for me. Her very favorite is gone, and her second favorite is good enough. "Tell me about Massachusetts."

I shift back and lean against a pine tree that scratches my back. "It's wet and cold and beautiful and small. And I love it. I—" I want to say that I had a million friends there, and that's kind of true, but also I haven't really been checked on by anyone outside the group chat.

Not that group chats don't count.

But also ... that it's not like I really had a best friend in Massachusetts. My best friends always switched around every few months and I never could hang on to anyone. Never found anyone I *wanted* to hang onto enough even if they did.

I always hated it—enough that I never let myself think about it, not until now in this cold moment stranded in the mountains. Like what the hell was so wrong with me that I didn't have a person I'd loved since the first grade to finish my sentences and go shopping for prom dresses with like it was a foregone conclusion?

I had a million friends.

But not A Friend. Not A Friend who wasn't someone else's more than they were mine.

So I say, "I miss it."

"It sucks," says Jolie. "Having to leave like that. Your senior year."

"Yeah." This close to the heels of a truth, the lie is a little less painful to tell. "All my friends, you know."

Jolie says, "At least you're starting school with me in a couple weeks! I'll introduce you to everyone. It's not—I know it's not the same ..."

I smile. "Yeah. That'll be good. Great. I'll be fine." I will. It will be good. I want to do this, I *want* to start school and hang out with her . . . with her . . . what kind of friends? I blink, realizing I can't exactly picture her hanging out at school, can't conjure who she hangs out with or what she even does at school, because my conversations with her have been limited to cozy one-on-ones at family Thanksgivings and Instagram comments.

At some point, Sam and Tzipporah have wandered over and Sam says, "You ought to, like, do a movie night before school starts up. With all your crazy theater friends. Hallie can be the mysterious cousin from the east."

Tzipporah says, "No no. Do *Rocky*! *Rocky Horror* niiight."

"Ugh," says Jolie. "You guys don't know my life."

Tzipporah says, "*Rocky Horror* night. And invite Yvette."

Jolie's pale cheeks pink and she says, "Dude, Yvette performs *Rocky Horror*, as though she'd want to come hang out in my janky basement and watch it *again*."

"Please," says Sam. "All that means is that it's the perfect film to make out during. She's already seen it."

"Ugh, godddddddd," says Jolie, but she's smiling.

And I'm hurt or something. Like how dare even Sam— not Tzipporah, *Tzipporah's girlfriend!*—know more about my own family than I do. I feel so lonely suddenly, like that's the biggest problem I have right now. But I feel lonely. I feel . . . cheated. I smile, like I can fix it, somehow catch up and regain all this ground I've lost by living two thousand miles away. I say, "Ooooh, who's Yvette?"

Jolie says, "No one!"

And Sam corrects: "Someone," with this smirk on her face.

Jolie rolls her eyes. "It's nothing. Just this girl in theater. She—I don't know. We're friends. She's one of the actors and she's so . . . perfect in, like, every single role. It's not like we're onstage together; I do tech. Anyway. We're friends." She digs her teeth into her lip.

I arch an eyebrow.

"You should . . ." Jolie blows out a breath and looks up at the cold, frosted sky. "You should see her hair, though. It's so blue and shiny. You should see her smile."

"I knew it!" says Tzipporah.

"UGH," says Jolie, falling backward dramatically, and for a second, I feel this flutter in my chest. Like, *look at me! She confessed to ME. Maybe I really am the favorite cousin. Maybe I mean to her what she does to me. Maybe I can . . . be part of this.*

I don't know.

My head sounds weird and desperate.

I am, for the second time today, so glad that telepathy isn't real.

Jolie jumps up and says, "Damn this ground. It's like rock."

"Of course it is; it's Colorado. You know that's, like, our number one flora," says Tzipporah.

I laugh.

Jolie says, "It's not *actual* rock. It's the ground. It's just . . . too cold."

And suddenly all of us are brought back to reality. To where we are.

To Lydia rolling her ankle and sucking back tears and

Oliver, who looks so, so young right now, warming his hands by the pile of warm ashes, eyeing the granola bars like he's about to stage a coup.

It's morning, dude! Get it together!

"How long do you think they'll be gone?" I say.

Jolie looks off toward the direction they left, worry sparking in her eyes. "Not long, I think."

What she means is: *I hope.*

We spend the rest of the day just kind of wandering around, trying to get warm, trying to comfort Lydia and Oliver, trying not to think about food.

Telling tiny snippets of stories here and there to distract ourselves.

Looking.

Looking, listening for any possible sign of Jaxon and Jonah.

We spend the day . . . waiting.

CHAPTER SEVEN

IT'S DARK.

Dark enough that I'd started to wonder if, like, a mountain lion had gotten them both. If Jaxon was off trying to wrestle a bear or Jonah was stuck in a ravine under a rock ready to gnaw his hand off.

And what a shame that would be to do to his perfect hands.

Ha ha.

Hilarious.

All of this is hilarious and appropriate to joke about.

Ha. Hahahahaha oh my god are they okay?

I'm standing at the edge of the not exactly campground, pacing, pine needles crunching under my feet and breath drifting out of my mouth like clouds. Clouds that come faster and faster as the time passes.

Maybe I should go look for them? My cell doesn't have much juice left, and it's totally useless for service, but it's got enough to use the flashlight function. And I'm trained in first aid; it makes more sense that I go to rescue them than anyone else.

Fine; it's fine. I can go tromping through the woods in the dark.

It's my responsibility, I think. For some reason.

I don't know why, except that it just . . . it just feels like *someone* needs to do it.

I keep pacing.

Hesitating.

Pulse choking me, breath dying in my lungs.

Then there's the crunch of leaves coming not from behind me, but from the fathomless dark in front of me.

I shrink back, operating on instinct—what if it's the bear? What if it's the bear that ate Jaxon and left Jonah stranded in that ravine and forced him to gnaw off his arm?

What if it's coming for its revenge?

I blink hard.

Jesus, I may need to go eat something.

Still, I fall back to the campfire—which we left Sam and Tzipporah to the challenge of starting. Only one of us (Jonah, Eagle Scout, surprise, surprise) brought a lighter. How the hell did I not bring a lighter, of all things? And Jolie brought some matches, but we're reserving those for more emergent situations. So the girls basically spent all day going back and forth debating a number of internet-tested methods I have mentally logged away. Eventually, they settled on a method that involved a can of Coke and a chocolate bar and a focused beam of light, which I think was just an excuse to snag a Coke and chocolate, but what are you gonna do? The point is it worked, and I'm finding my way back to the familiar warmth and light.

Away from whatever murder-bear-ghost is coming at me in the dark.

"Jacob," I hear, and Jonah's voice about buckles my knees.

"Oh, thank god," I say, and I break out toward them in a run.

I don't throw my arms around Jonah—that would be weird—but I practically tackle Jaxon.

"SHIT," I say, punching him hard in the arm.

He flinches. "What the hell?"

"I thought you were dead. Do you know how long it's been? And you!" I say to Jonah. "Thank god, your hand."

He smirks and says, "Oh come on, Hal—wait, I'm sorry, what?"

Then I realize what I said, but it doesn't matter. What matters is that they're okay and they're back and maybe, *maybe* they're back with information.

Slowly, the rest of the cousins (and crew) begin to notice the commotion, and they crowd around the fire. Most of them have been here since the sun dipped.

There's excited chatter from everyone, like now that we've sent our best and brightest out, we won't have to resort to cannibalism to survive.

This is it: the daring moment of escape, the reveal of the getaway vehicle, the teary sighting of help landing over the ridge, rising with the sun.

"So," says Jaxon, running his hand over his stubble-sprinkled jaw. "So, okay, I don't . . . I don't want anyone to panic."

The mood darkens considerably.

Quickly.

So quick it feels like the sky is suddenly crushing down on my shoulders, like *physical* night has descended and decided to push me into the earth.

Jonah is standing beside Jaxon, arms folded. He looks tall, looks kind of giant even though he isn't *that* big, not really. He just holds authority in his stance. Holds . . . our future, really. Like when Jaxon spoke, he gave all our hope to Jonah Ramirez.

Jaxon looks at him, face all pleading.

Jonah would take care of it.

He always did, didn't he?

Since they were little, Jaxon's been getting into shit and Jonah's been getting him out.

Jaxon: diving into the lake without a life jacket at nine years old the time we all decided to meet up at Lake Powell in the summer.

Jonah: furiously ripping off his Ninja Turtles T-shirt and tossing in a life preserver and going in after him when—SURPRISE—it turned out Jaxon was a shitty swimmer. Jonah was not.

Jaxon: trying to sneak off with some skis that were supposed to be rentals when he was thirteen, getting caught by a grumpy old security guard who was having a very bad day already.

Jonah: sweet talking the grumpy old security guard, somehow wrangling two free day passes he pocketed (he'd earned them) and Jaxon not like . . . going to juvie or getting banned for life from the mountain or whatever it is they do to seventh-grade ski gear thieves who don't have a Jonah to stand up for them.

Jaxon: getting caught by my parents with weed at Fancy Snowy Ridge at sixteen.

Jonah: taking the blame, getting a total earful from my dad, almost getting his trip privileges taken away, never actually telling Jaxon what happened.

That last one twinges something in me.

My dad—my parents always twinge.

I ignore it.

The point is, Jonah always takes care of everything, now that I really let myself think about it. And so of course we all know he will take care of this now.

Jaxon is fidgeting, looking for some kind of purchase, some way to say whatever he needs to say. And the harder he struggles looking for it, the more restless we all get.

Jaxon blows out a shaky breath in the quiet and eventually open his mouth to continue, and Jonah just sighs.

He says, over the obvious relief in Jaxon's eyes, "No truck. No truck, no car, no sign of it. We couldn't find any of our trail markers, but that's not a surprise. None of it is a surprise. It was worth a shot, we took it, and now we can rest easy knowing we did what we could today."

"Rest *easy?*" says Oliver. Oliver, I know, is Lydia's best friend and it's good he's here and I've always liked him, but he can be a little exhausting sometimes, just a little . . . I don't know. Concernicus. Now is of course the time for concern in all forms, but for some reason that probably has to do with panic and cold and hunger, it feels like *Jesus, of course it's Oliver with the smartass C-3PO commentary.*

"Well," says Jonah, "rest like shit."

I rub my curled fingers over my own knee. Over and over. Hard and fast enough I think the jeans might ignite.

No truck. No SUV. No trail. No nothing.

Okay.

Sure.

Alright.

This is fine.

This. Is fine.

Jonah says, "No-panic rule still applies. We can't be that far from the vehicles; we're not, like, lost in the middle of the Himalayas in the dead of winter, no rescue in sight. The fact is that in one direction or another, we can't be that far from the road. We're close enough to town. It's going to be fine."

I shudder and hug my coat around me. The fire only does so much against the dry Colorado cold.

I can feel the pink in the tip of my nose.

I can feel the panic everywhere else.

I try, I physically try, to slow my pulse and warm myself at the same time.

I don't know that I can reasonably ask for both.

I'm cold.

I'm *cold I'm hungry I'm cold.*

FUCK.

Fuck, we are TRAPPED.

I lean forward, elbows digging into my knees, hoping the sharp pain of my bones on my own bones will snap me back from the rising fear.

That's not what does it.

What does it is the sudden gulping I hear coming from the other side of the fire.

It sounds like someone is sucking air through a straw, a straw that's cracked at the bottom.

I look up and it's Sam. She clutching her throat and Tzipporah is suddenly down on the ground, hands on either side of Sam's face, and Sam is losing it.

Shit.

"Sam?" I say.

I click, from Regular Allowed To Freak Out Hallie to Paramedic I Live to Fight Fires Hallie. I cannot let my fear own me, and in this immediate, effortless shift, I don't even know how I would.

I'm not even shaking anymore; I'm completely calm.

I say, "Sam," and elbow my way past all of my cousins on the way to her.

The only person I don't straight up shove is Tzipporah, because the girl she loves might have a better shot at calming her than I do.

I kneel beside Tzipporah and yell back over my shoulder to the group, "Shut up. SHUT UP. Shut the FUCK up," and the camp goes silent.

"Pursed lips," I say to Sam, and Sam's panicked eyes find me. They're wide and bloodshot and her face is going a little blue. With the cold? With the lack of air? Both?

Everything in my brain zeroes. I am not cold, I am not worried, I am not panicked. I am focused. I see: her face. I feel: the rhythm of her breathing. I hear: the shallow breaths.

I don't even blink.

"Pursed lips," I say again, and this time it's a total command.

Sam struggles into it and I say, "In through your nose."

She tries. The sound is horrible.

"Sit straight up and in through your nose. Now. Out through those pursed lips. Breathe out twice as long. Keep going."

Tzipporah is whispering to her, hands gentle and strong at once on her face, and I'm still playing bad cop over here. But she's listening.

She's listening, and after a minute, two, the color enters her face again and she starts to breathe. It's ragged at first, and then just shallow. Then finally, finally, it returns, more or less, to normal.

No one moves a muscle.

No one knows what to say.

Until Jaxon offers, "Panic attack?"

"Asthma," says Sam. Her voice comes out rough, like her trachea is a little bruised.

I frown. "Do you . . . did you not bring your inhaler?"

"Of course I did; I'm not fucking stupid," Sam snaps, and I flinch.

Then she breathes again, quiet and slow. She says, "Sorry. I'm sorry." She looks hard at me, an apology that's not really necessary written on her face. "I just mean, yeah, I brought it. But we lost it in the mudslide."

"That didn't trigger an attack?"

"Yeah. Got it taken care of before anyone noticed but Tzipporah. I'm fine. Don't worry about me."

"Well," I say, "shit."

A chorus of "Well, shit"'s replies to me.

"I'm *fine*," she grumbles, leaning into Tzipporah. "You really want to help me, someone find me some lotion for this ashy skin." Tzipporah pets her hair lightly and Sam runs her hands over her arms.

She's not fine, and I know it. And so does she.

I hate this.

"Listen," says Jonah, "I hate to do the *calm down, all you overreactors* thing? But we all do need to remain calm. Hopefully a couple days of smoke is enough to signal search parties to our area. And if not, we're going to figure it out in the morning."

Sam's ragged breathing plays in my head, scratches as it pulses through my veins.

We'll figure it out.

We have until morning.

Because Sam can breathe.

Well.

She can breathe *now*.

God, this is a fucking nightmare.

CHAPTER EIGHT

AT THIS POINT, I start to think that no one is coming.

No one is coming because we are all absolutely *stupid*.

It was so monumentally stupid coming out here all alone, not telling anyone where we were going, leaving no hint whatsoever as to our whereabouts. Like we're a bunch of punk kids who've never been in the mountains before. You always, always tell someone where you're going.

I rub my fist over my burning, tired eyes, and it comes away salty and wet.

I can't believe I'm crying. I can't waste the water. You wouldn't think that would really be much of an issue when you're literally surrounded by water, but the problem is that that water is frozen. Consuming enough snow to fill the tank is a good way to get hypothermia and freeze yourself to death from the inside out.

So no. No, it is, in fact, an issue, and I absolutely shouldn't be using the energy or the water on crying.

I sniff, too-thin gloves coming away cold and wet from my nose.

I don't even think I'm sad. I'm just so mad. I'm so mad

that we did this, that I did this. I'm furious and, unfortunately, I'm an angry crier. So here I am, hot and mad and leaking out of my face.

There's nothing more infuriating than this—being a short girl absolutely ripping someone's ass, and then feeling the heat behind your eyes so you're trying to be scary, but now congrats—you can't. You're too mad.

You're sobbing.

I'm not sobbing; I have it at least that much under control.

But I am livid, and so I am crying.

I take several deep breaths, following my own advice to Sam.

I stand when I think I can face everyone, and my eyes find Lydia, who at this point is just lying there on her side, quietly weeping. Jolie is sitting behind her, petting her hair and whispering shushing sounds to her.

I say, "That ankle?"

Lydia nods, eyes squeezed tight against the pain. "Slept on it wrong," she says. "Got up to pee and . . ." She doesn't finish it.

I meet Jolie's eyes.

Neither of us says a thing.

I wonder if she's thinking about Sam from last night like I am.

I wonder if she's thinking about how impossible it would be to take care of our wounded, littlest cousin if something wild came out of that brush and got a little brave, like I am.

I wonder if she's thinking: *No one's coming. It's save ourselves or nobody will.*

Like I am.

I can't stop thinking about it, about Sam going the palest, most alarming shade of brown, about the absolute terror in Tzipporah's eyes, like I've never seen before, not on her.

I can't stop thinking about the pressure, the urgency, the sudden realization that Sam could die here.

Not in the abstract, *We're all in a bad situation here! We could die!* kind of way. In the real, solid, brush it with your fingers kind of way.

Sam, who's loved my beautiful, pain in the ass, incredible cousin Tzipporah for two years, could die up here.

She could have died last night.

And who knows what's happening with Lydia. Is it a break or a sprain or an infection or . . .

What I know is it's not getting any better.

It's sure as hell not increasing her odds of survival.

It's not increasing any of ours.

I am high on lack of sleep, on absolute fury at this whole situation, on bone-deep fear that I won't be able to protect the people I care about—not from here.

It is not rationale speaking for me when I suddenly stand and say, "I'm leaving."

There's a blanket of quiet for several seconds.

Jonah says, "Come again?"

I turn to face him, eyes flashing. "I'm leaving. Sam's sick and Lydia's hurt and I just think someone needs to."

"Needs to what?" he says. He's relaxing against his log, because of course he is. Looking lazy and challenging which, once again, of course.

"Find help."

"How the hell are you going to find help?" he says. "This is an abandoned mountain, dude. Jaxon and I ran it yesterday and there's no one. There's nothing. Just snow and rock and mud and destruction for days."

"So WHAT?" I say. "I'm supposed to just sit here? Just sit here and wait for help to come too late?"

Jonah scoffs. "It's a dumbass decision and you know it. Every time a couple bodies get picked up outside a crashed car in the wilderness, it's because they decided to leave their vehicle. Smart people don't do this."

I bristle at that attempted manipulation. Those tears pop up hot and sharp behind my eyes and I blink them back. No. Not now. Absolutely not. Every protest just makes my resolve stronger. I curl my hands into fists at my sides and go for my backpack, leaving out what I think should be left at camp, packing what needs to come with me. "Anyone who wants to come," I say, "can come with me. I'm trained in paramedics and I'm confident we can work together to do this as . . . as safely as possible."

Jonah just snorts and Jaxon peers at me. "Splitting up, Hallie? That just . . . it's never the way to go," Jaxon says.

"It is now," I say. "Don't you GET IT? Don't any of you get it? She could die! Sam could DIE."

Tzipporah flinches at the thought, arm curling around Sam protectively.

Sam tightens her fingers on Tzipporah's leg but that's it.

"Lydia has something really wrong, too. And what if no one finds us before it can be fixed? Hmm? Someone has to get back. You don't have to be brave; none of you do. No one has to follow me. I can go. I can . . . I can do this on my own if I need to."

"Don't," says Tzipporah.

Jolie joins her, and I say, "Someone has to. SOMEONE HAS TO."

I can feel the weight and the echo all around me.

Someone has to.

I let it hang.

No one else wants to.

I look around the circle, suddenly terrified. I don't actually know if I *can* do this alone; I was trying to prove a point.

"We should stay, Hal," says Sam.

I clench my teeth. "You stay. All of you, if you want."

"Don't, Hallie. Please. You can't go on your *own* out there."

"If I don't," I say, "who will?"

I zip up my bag.

No one tries to, like, physically restrain me or anything.

They tell me not to do this, ask me not to, almost beg me not to.

But no one holds me back.

I don't know why that stings, but I have to go.

Maybe it's because they know I have to.

And they're all too chickenshit.

Well, that's not fair. Jaxon would never leave Jolie. If she came, so would he. Oliver is young. Sam is sick and Tzipporah should stay with her, and Lydia, obviously, should *definitely* not come along.

Everyone thinks I'm dumb.

Or they're lazy.

Or they're . . . I don't know.

I don't know.

I know this goes against what every expert tells you to do when you're lost. I know that.

But every expert didn't see Sam choking on her own lungs last night.

Every expert didn't watch Lydia get worse and worse until she couldn't freaking move.

Every expert hasn't sat here for two days freezing to death on a mountain known for allowing people to disappear in *oppressive,* lonely silence, knowing deep in their heart that help isn't coming.

I am not every expert.

But I am here.

And I am doing what needs to be done.

I give it twenty minutes, to be sure I have what I need. To check and recheck my pack, divvy out first aid supplies, leaving most of them for the people who are already hurt, taking just a couple small items for myself. A little tube of antibiotic cream. Bandages. That kind of thing.

And then, well. I leave.

People are done making their moves to convince me, and I can't help but wonder if it's because I'm the weakest link, the kid from Massachusetts who they never see anyway.

I choke that down and stomp it out.

What matters is none of that.

What matters is surviving.

For all of us.

That is the assurance I force to play in my head over and over as I go alone into the quiet woods.

Snow sprinkles the ground, in piles and sprays and drifts. It smells like wintertime, all pine and frostbitten air, if the winter were utterly lonely and menacing when it came.

It's not like I'm paying much attention to the ground, but I don't see tracks—the only ones here are mine. Everything is sleeping for the winter or so small and scarce that they don't need to litter the entire ground with tracks, don't need to compete for space.

I don't see any rabbits or foxes or hear a single bird.

It's unsettling, the lack of noise that comes so immediately after I leave. The snow blanket mutes everything I should hear, which, in these woods, isn't much.

It's eerie, just listening to the almost-nothing breeze, my own footsteps.

That's it.

That's all it's going to be for who knows how long.

I sink into the cold quiet.

Five minutes out of camp, I hear a crunching behind me. It's rhythmic and fast, and the telltale swish of cheap, thick ski gear gives it away.

I stop where I am.

I let him catch up.

"What do you want?" I say.

I don't look at him. I just say it to the path ahead of me.

He says, "I'm not letting you go alone."

I say, "You think you could stop me, Jonah?"

Jonah sighs, and in the quiet, I do look at him.

He says, "I'm not stopping you."

I raise an eyebrow.

"She's hurt. Lydia. And Sam last night. And you're taking off out here like you're Wonder Woman or some shit, and I think if anyone tried to stop you now, you'd just sneak off in the middle of the night, wouldn't you?"

I shrug.

Probably.

"So go. Before I change my mind."

I stay rooted in the spot.

"Goddammit, Jacob," he says. He stands a little taller, muscle in his cheek twitching. "*Go.*"

I take another second with all of it, nerves and fear and dread and comfort settling at once into my stomach. I take in the set of Jonah's jaw, the dark, furious determination in his eyes that invites no argument. I swallow.

And I walk off.

He keeps pace.

After the silence falls for just a little too long to be comfortable, I say, "I thought you said smart people didn't do this."

He breathes, and for a second, all I hear are his exhales and the crunch of snow beneath our feet.

Then he says, "Well, I must be really fucking stupid."

And we leave them all for the wild.

CHAPTER NINE

JONAH NOT-SO-QUIETLY LET ME know I was heading in what was probably the wrong direction, based on what he and Jaxon had found out the day before, and we'd changed course—westward it was.

I tried to pretend like that didn't bug me, like it didn't grate that the first thing I'd done on my own was screw up. But that's what I get, I guess, for not having a plan. This is what we all get.

Unlike the entire incident, though, I guess there really was no way to plan for this. For the rescue trip—a trek across the Rockies in the dead of winter wherein the whole mountainside has just been torn apart. That's what I hate, I think: knowing that I *can't* plan. I can't get a hold of any kind of strategy that isn't just . . . wandering. Any plan is going to come ten seconds into a disaster, a reaction. I can't see the potential events or paths in front of me, so how could I possibly choose one?

I grit my teeth.

I have to keep going.

And I hate it.

That's what's making me crazy.

Jonah glances back at me, over his shoulder, and says, "You doing okay?"

"Fine," I say.

He arches an eyebrow. "You sure? Because you look kind of . . ." He passes his hand over his face in a vague gesture and grimaces.

"Kind of what?" I say. It comes out like a growl.

"Just. Grumpy."

"*Grumpy*? Oh Jesus, not *grumpy*! I'm so sorry, Jonah, what can I do for you to make your stay in the fucking Arctic more comfortable?"

He rolls his eyes and turns around, shoving his hands deep into his pockets. "Fine. Quiet Lyft rides are the best ones anyway."

I think I actually snort out loud. It's a little hard to tell through the cold in my nose, but the immediate derision needs somewhere to escape. I scoff again through my mouth to be certain it's been noted aloud, and then I powerwalk to keep up with him.

"It's your legs," I say.

He deadpans, "My legs."

"I can't keep up with you on those tree trunks, you absolute giraffe, and I'm tired."

"You can't be tired yet; we've got a whole-ass mountain to cover. And I'll slow down, Christ. I should have volunteered to go in your place."

"Oh," I say, sarcasm seeping into my voice, "how romantic."

He barks out a laugh. "Trust me. Not romantic."

I narrow my eyes, still struggling just a little to keep up even after he's allegedly slowed down, and say, "You were about to shove your tongue down my throat before the landslide hit."

"Well, circumstances change."

When I say "Like?" I expect him to respond with something about the reorganization of the landscape, which will give me the perfect lead-in to explain what I think should be the pretty obvious source of my grumpiness.

But when I say "Like?" he says, "Like your being really fucking annoying."

"Excuse me?" I say.

"You asked."

"I'm not being annoying."

His eyebrows hit his hairline and he just keeps moving. "Okay."

My nose wrinkles. I don't know why this is even bothering me; he's being a jerk. We're setting off on a mission to save our own lives and the lives of our friends and family; this is petty. Of both of us, really.

But . . . *annoying?* How am I even being annoying?

It can't be the grumpy thing—can it?

I feel the urge to explain myself, and I hate that I want to explain myself at all. I don't owe him.

And yet.

I find myself opening my mouth and saying, "It's not just your legs. It's this whole thing. It's freezing and I'm scared for everyone, not least of all *us*, and this was so freaking impulsive which isn't like me at all, and we don't even have a map! We have no working knowledge of the area, Jonah! We have ZERO plan."

He stops right there and turns around.

Her grabs my arms, and I can feel the pinpoints of his fingertips through my coat. My eyes widen and my pulse spikes, and a muscle in his jaw jumps.

He breathes—in through his nose. Out. Like he's consciously trying to calm himself down. He says, "Hallie."

"What?"

"We are hiking across a mountain."

"Yes."

"In the dead of winter."

I take a breath. "Mmhmm."

He pulls me just an inch closer. "This is an extremely fucking stressful situation."

"Y-yes."

"Do you understand that you losing your goddamn shit is not helping that?"

I'm shaking. My breath is shaking. "Y-yes."

He just stares at me, so hard I cannot look away. His eyes are so dark, so freaking intense. I don't know how I've never noticed how totally tangible it is when he looks at you. Like he's speaking.

He says, "So can you please, *please* just like . . . be quiet? For nine seconds?"

I don't know why that strikes me as funny, but it does.

Something makes me laugh.

Then I am losing it, right bicep still caught in his grip, just cackling, laughter echoing through the silent trees.

He doesn't laugh, but after a few seconds, after I'm literally crying a little bit, his mouth quirks up.

"You good?" he says.

"Yeah." I wipe a couple freezing tears from my eyes. "Yeah, I'm good."

"Okay." He drops my arm and backs up a pace.

"Okay."

"Jonah."

He breathes again, slowly, intentionally, and glances up at the clear blue sky. "Yes?"

"We need to make a plan."

The longest pause of the century.

"Jesus Christ."

I try to lock eyes with him; I'm certain I could transmit the necessity of what I'm saying to him through osmosis if I could just get him to look at me. He would see reason if he would stare into my eyes.

I say, "I'm doing this for your own good. Unless you want to die up here. Is that what you want?"

He looks at me.

Jackpot.

He says, "Of course it's not."

"Then we need a plan." I smile smugly; everything that has transpired has done so according to my design. The eye lock has clenched it. He is seeing reason.

He furrows his brow and the moment before he speaks, I see that I was in error. "How, exactly?" he says. "How exactly do you intend to lay one? We're surrounded on all sides by snow and rock and trees that all look the same."

I say, "I thought you knew this mountain."

"I know it like a dude knows places you go to get high. Every time I've been here, I've been stoned."

"So?" I say. "Pink Floyd wrote their best stuff stoned."

He laughs. "Ah, yes, writing trippy shit about English boarding schools. Exactly the same skill set required for topnotch cartographers."

"I'm just saying it didn't completely blow your ability to think, did it?"

Jonah has been pretty rock solid and chill, but now he's blustering. He's gesturing widely—not wildly, but wide enough for me to note is bordering on wild for him. "No, but that doesn't change the fact that I don't know the place like the back of my hand, man. I've been up here enough times I might, I *might* recognize a valley or a peak or a weird ring of trees, enough to get us back, which is more than I can say for anyone but Jaxon so it . . . it could come in handy. But I'm not going to start spouting off shit like *Turn left at that lightning-struck pine tree. Head straight at the grizzly bear.*"

I roll my eyes, smiling despite the situation. Then I hear what he said, fully process it. "I'm sorry—grizzly bear? Are there . . . are there grizzlies here?"

"Nah," he says. "Black bears, but you'd be surprised at how small those dudes are."

"Really?"

"Like four and a half feet. You're taller than a black bear."

"Oh," I say. "Well, huh."

"Yup." Jonah cocks his head, sizes me up. "Okay, you're not *much* taller."

I wrinkle my nose. "Excuse you; I'm five foot four."

"Tiny," he says.

I'm not even tiny! I wouldn't call myself small, either, and neither does anyone else. But I guess I don't often hang out with dudes as big as Jonah.

Still.

I huff.

We're walking again, somehow, which goes against my plans, but we'll circle back to that. I say, "So I don't have to worry about them then."

He doesn't look back at me; he's zoned in on the non-path of white and brush and open sky ahead. "About what?"

"The bears."

"Oh, no, they'll still totally eat you."

I choke.

"It would just be more like getting killed by a raptor than a T-rex."

"Oh my *god*," I say.

He looks back over his shoulder. "Keep up, shortstop."

"If a bear comes out of these woods, I'm tripping you."

I still make an effort to keep step with him.

"Relax," he says. "Number one: bears are terrified of people. You just have to stand there, look huge, and yell. They'll run the hell away. Unless it's a sow. You get between a sow and her cubs, you're asking to be eaten. So just don't do that. Number two: they're all hibernating anyway. It's winter."

"Oh. Right." My pulse falls back to a survivable level. "You could have led with that," I grumble.

"Sorry, I thought the snow made that clear. And also the December."

"The *bear thing*, jackass."

He's got that insufferable (or well . . . *something*-able) perma-smirk on his face. "This is fun, though."

I groan. "Well. At least I don't have to worry about things with sharp teeth."

He smiles with his.

I almost trip.

"Well. Not bears," he says. "It's the mountain lions you gotta watch for."

"Are you serious?"

"Yeah. They kill people out here every year."

"Holy shit."

He shrugs. "You see one of those fuckers, you stand your ground. Make yourself big. You don't run, because you can trigger their instinct to chase you. There's ways to protect yourself if they come at you, which I can show you if you're—"

"No," I say. I don't know why that thought is so unnerving to me, but it is, and I just desperately don't want to deal with it right now. It seems too immediate, too real, too exposed out here in the open woods.

The woods, even this deep in, aren't crowded enough to feel like they provide any cover. Even in the aspen clusters, if you lost track of your dog, you could see her run for a couple hundred yards before she disappeared. It feels so wide open. Barren. Utterly, gratingly vulnerable.

I'm afraid of mountain lions, I'm afraid of hibernating bears, god I'm afraid of large enough *hawks* swooping down to snatch me into the air right now; it's too real.

And it's stupid.

But the last thing my nerves can handle right now is talk of defense against a predator.

He just says, "Okay. Well, let me know if you change your mind."

I say, "Okay."

And I follow him.

I take in the less immediate surroundings, the rocks that jut up from the earth like giants. They're beautiful in such a different, more terrifying way than any of the beauty in New England. They aren't dead; they've never been *living*. Somehow that makes them more terrifying, less human, even, than the trees. The scenery here is rock.

It is sharp.

It is desolate.

The rocks are red and brown and the scar of the slide crashes through everything; it's hard to tell what lies the way it does because it's used to it and what is split because of an act of G-d.

I keep staring until it's familiar. Like a focal point when you're trying to balance on one leg. Until the mountain is what's keeping me grounded.

"What if . . ."

Jonah lets out a long, audible sigh. "Mmhmm?"

"What if we head for that peak?"

"Why?"

I shrug. "Something to aim for."

Jonah stares off at it, then squints up into the bright sky. "Well, that peak is west at least, and Old Snowy Ridge is east of New. So, I mean, okay. Makes more sense than anything else."

I nod and we shift direction slightly.

Suddenly, I feel like I can fall into a rhythm. Like this isn't just random chaos, like death isn't a total inevitability. I feel like I'm in control of something.

Like if we reach that peak, I could check it off in my mental bullet journal and move on to the next task.

And that matters.

When the snow begins to fall from the sky in quiet, cold little flakes, I keep my eyes on that peak.

Eventually, *eventually*, it will get closer.

CHAPTER TEN

I KIND OF FEEL? Like it doesn't?

I say to Jonah, "I kind of feel like that mountain is not getting closer."

Jonah says, "Well. It better be."

I say, "How is it possible that it looks as far away now as it did two hours ago?"

"I'm so hungry."

"I'm thirsty."

Jonah says, "Man, we're being whiners. It's not even the afternoon."

I laugh, but it comes out just a little cry-y.

"You ever think about that?" he says, marching resolutely forward to the magically non-growing mountain.

"Think about what?"

"How just like ... ridiculous our problems are? Like, last week I was playing *Fortnite* with Jax and—"

"*Jax?*"

"Shut up, yes, Jax."

I snicker.

"And my screen started glitching, and I didn't land a

shot I should have and Jax lived and ganked me and I was so furious. Legit, I was composing the most strongly worded email to customer service before I remembered that the customer service rep is probably some nineteen-year-old like me who doesn't get paid enough for this shit and dialed it down, and then I just lividly shut off my laptop and sat there thinking about how irritated I was for five minutes. Like, how dare this happen to me."

"Stable."

"But like . . . what would a Viking have to say about that shit?"

"What?"

"You know, like if a Viking showed up and I was like, *FUCK, Jorgenvalder. I've had a DAY, man,* and walked him through this problem, he'd probably just pitch me into the ocean. His bad day consisted of his village burning down and some pirates raiding his ship."

I spit out a laugh. "I don't think Vikings and pirates coexisted."

"Well, a pirate would have similar sympathies for me."

"Prehistoric human, help. My iPhone has not been updated for days."

"BIG FUCKING DEAL, MY WIFE GOT EATEN BY A MAMMOTH."

I'm laughing so hard, I bet my face is red. I mean, it's cold; it was probably already red.

I say, when I can take a breath, "You: deeply concerned that your Totino's pizza rolls are cold on the outside but somehow lava on the inside. A dude in Pompeii: eyeing that volcano *really* suspiciously."

He's laughing, too, that husky laugh that sounds so . . . so absurdly sexy I don't know how it's real. Don't know how it's not rehearsed.

Don't know how I'm even thinking about that right now.

The snow crusts up around my shoes, and I'm so glad I didn't wear canvas sneakers like I usually do. Even still, it's cold. Even still, it's a reminder that this isn't just a hike with someone I'm not supposed to hike with.

I almost forgot that for a half a second.

I think maybe I could forget about it for a few seconds longer if I really wanted.

I say, "You know, Vikings actually hated hiking."

He raises an eyebrow. "Yeah?"

"Yes. They would do practically anything to avoid climbing. They have legends of meeting with rulers in the middle of landlocked Asia—*by boat*—because any place worth going could obviously be reached by boat."

He's not saying much, he's just kind of . . . almost smiling, but not quite.

I continue: "They would just sail around any place that required climbing. No matter how much longer it took."

"Mm," he says.

"So what I'm saying is, if you told Jorgenvalder that today sucked, Jorgenvalder would probably say, *IT DOES SUCK, JONAH RAMIREZ. FUCK THIS MOUNTAIN. WHERE IS MY BOAT.*"

He does laugh, then. "So you're a nerd then."

"Excuse me?"

"I'm learning things."

"About Vikings?"

He smiles. After years of four-second glances and eaves-dropping on him and Jaxon and Jolie and thinking about what it might be like to be near him, I still don't know him well enough to know if the smile is totally sincere. What does sincere look like on him?

I stop wondering about the minutiae of his face.

He says, through that smile that's probably at least half real, "About you."

My throat tightens, just the smallest bit.

"I'm not that much of a nerd," I say.

"No? How do you know so much about Vikings?"

I look prim and march forward. "Knowledge is power, Jonah."

"Nerd," he says, and I'm so turned around.

What we have here is nearly a rapport. It's suddenly almost easy, suddenly like we haven't been getting on each other's last nerve all day. It's suddenly like I'm ... glad I'm not doing this on my own.

I swing my backpack around and pull out a couple granola bars, then toss one to him.

"Thanks," he says, and I unpeel mine.

We eat in cold, companionable silence, making our way toward the mountain peak.

The breeze is light, thank god, and the sun rises higher in the sky so that it almost, *almost* feels warm. I bite into the granola bar, and only then does it become clear to me how hungry I am. There's a pang in my stomach, and it twists—hollow and solid all at once. I can feel the sudden weakness in my limbs, the desperate gnawing under my skin.

"Jesus," I mutter.

I can't decide whether I want to devour the thing in two bites or make it last.

I want both.

Jonah glances over at me and chews.

I can feel myself start to weaken, which seems so counter to what ingesting calories should be doing to me right now, but *god*, suddenly hiking any farther seems impossible.

I breathe.

I chew.

It no longer feels like a fun extracurricular, a hike on a crisp winter's day.

It feels like I'm hungry.

It feels like we're lost.

Jonah clears his throat. "Hey," he says, "what do you know?"

I glance up.

"That peak is finally getting closer."

I focus on the mountain, which only an hour ago seemed impossibly far away.

And he's right.

He's right.

We are going to make it.

Dusk is beginning to fall when we start the *real* ascent. I would have sworn, based on the burn in my lungs and my muscles, the utter exhaustion every step I took, that we had started it hours ago, but I would have been wrong.

This is the real deal.

Suddenly, my plan seems so stupid.

Why did we decide to climb this mountain in the first place? How is getting higher helpful at all? A vantage point, I guess.

Or something.

A goal—I need a goal. I need X to mark the spot and a number of steps to achieve that, or I think I would lose my mind.

I stripped off my thin gloves an hour ago because they were wet and freezing, but now my hands are getting pink and cracked in the dry cold. I clench my fists and unclench them.

I breathe—in through my nose, out through my mouth. In through my nose, out through my mouth.

There is nowhere to go from here but backward or up.

I'm lightheaded. The blood feels like it's rushing through my veins, like it's too fast and too thin and insubstantial. Like my heart is beating just a little too hard.

"You okay?" says Jonah.

"I'm fine," I snap, like his checking on me is an insult or something. Like he's implying I'm more out of shape than he is, which he's not trying to do. I'm just tired and I'm hungry, and by hungry, I mean *hangry*.

He says, "Sounds like it," totally unfazed.

"I'm just feeling a little weird," I say. "Probably tired."

Jonah narrows his eyes. "Weird how?"

"Just tired," I say.

"Just tired."

I shrug. I'm weirdly embarrassed; he's fine, why shouldn't I be?

"Talk to me," he says.

"Sorry, talking to you isn't exactly something I'm used to."

His tone is totally casual, conversational, but it's full of authority. I don't really know how it can be so deeply both. "Well, suck it up, princess. Talk. To me."

"I'm just kind of lightheaded," I say. "My pulse is sort of freaking out, but like I said, I'm fine. Don't worry about it; I'm probably just out of shape."

Jonah stops, and I stop with him. "Are you dizzy?"

"Not really. Kind of."

He makes this concerned, almost growly noise in the back of his throat and reaches out for me, fingers a loop around my wrist.

He slips them under my coat, and then my sleeves, so his cool fingers are pressed against my skin, and my breath hitches.

He's so focused I don't think he notices.

Thank god, because I am so acutely aware of the calluses on his fingertips, rough against the soft inner skin of my wrist, the intentional grip as he presses into the bones. I'm . . . shaking?

He says, "Shit."

"What?" I look up at him, and his hand is still pressing red into my skin.

"You're right; your pulse is like a jackrabbit's."

I swallow hard.

"You might have altitude sickness."

It takes me a second to process what he's saying, to recalibrate my brain. "Oh—wait, I might what?"

"Aren't you an EMT?"

Once again, I'm defensive. I say, "Training to be one. But in Massachusetts; we don't have *altitude* there, you asshole."

His fingers shift around my wrist, from his thumb pressing into my veins to all of them curling. It's a little possessive, almost. Protective, or something. I can feel the rough slip of skin on skin all the way down into my stomach.

"It . . . it can be kind of bad."

I keep looking at his eyes, because that scares me. And if I stay focused on the fact that there is another human here, maybe I won't panic. At whatever the hell "kind of bad" means.

"Okay . . ." I say.

"We probably need to just stop."

My stomach twists again, but it feels very different this time. Feels like total, instant panic. I don't want to stop. I want to reach that peak. Because then the goal is achieved, the plan has been conquered; we've done something today.

If we stop here, we've . . . we've failed. And it's my fault.

It's like the whole day is wasted.

That's not even logical, I know it's not, even as my racing brain tells me that it doesn't matter, it's the most reasonable thing in the world. Tells me that it makes complete sense to lose my mind over not hitting this stupid, arbitrary goal.

My eyes fill with tears, because I can't stop them.

I hate this.

I *hate* this.

I hate that my voice is ridiculously, nonsensically strangled when I say, "No. No, why? We don't need to stop."

He peers at me, thumb gentling around my arm. "We should, Hallie. Altitude sickness can literally kill you."

"What?" My voice comes out quiet, resigned in a way I don't want to be.

The dizziness picks up until I think I might actually fall over. Maybe it's altitude sickness. It's probably just this overwhelming sense of failure! I'm probably just exhausted!

"You've gone too high too fast, and you're dehydrated and hungry, and your body doesn't know what to do up here. I promise you, people have died from this."

A noise of frustration bubbles up in my throat and I stare at the ground. "I don't want to stop," I whisper.

"Why not?"

"Because," I say, "we have to make it to the top. That's the plan, Jonah. That's what we've been working toward all day."

"So?"

I look back up into his dark eyes and then pointedly at my own wrist.

He follows my gaze down and drops me like he's just touched fire.

"So? So, if we don't make it there . . ."

I can't finish the sentences because I know I'm being crazy. I know he'll look at me like I'm being nuts, because there's no reason I should need this.

Surprise, surprise. I am crazy, but only according to, you know, medical records.

Sweet, sweet anxiety.

Of course I'm being crazy! I'm being me.

He says, even and low, voice like a meditation, "If we don't make it there tonight, we can make it there tomorrow. Or reroute."

I blow out a shaky breath. "I hate this."

"You'll hate dying worse."

"That's so fucking dramatic."

He shrugs a shoulder and says, "Listen. Follow me. We're heading into those trees. We're finding some semblance of shelter, and we're parking for the night. You need to rest, man. I'm not bullshitting you, okay?"

Goddammit.

I purse my lips.

I don't say *Okay*. I don't acknowledge the failure verbally at all.

I just follow him into the shadows and let myself be led.

CHAPTER ELEVEN

JONAH REFUSES TO LET me help gather kindling.

He insists that I lie on the pine-needled ground, focusing on getting my shit together, focusing on breathing and not dying, however the hell I'm supposed to do that.

So I'm . . . doing that, I guess.

I try to think myself into hydration, my pulse into submission. I try very pointedly not to be dizzy.

I stare up through the pine boughs at the sky, streaked with blood and citrus.

I've collected my extremities in this big coat, as much as I can, and I've been horizontal for twenty minutes.

I'm getting cold, lying still, but Jonah said not moving was the best thing for me right now, and I guess I believe him. I kind of have to.

He's crouched over a pile of pine needles and dead aspen leaves—all this detritus he's gathered—trying to get it to catch. Jonah came with that lighter, thankfully, so the real struggle here is not the initial flame; it's just getting this not-optimally-dry tinder to light.

I can hear him blowing and crackling his way through

the stuff, coaxing it into keeping us warm. My teeth are chattering, and I wonder if Jonah can hear them, if it's spurring him further into action.

"EUREKA," he says, and I see him jump up and pump a fist in the air. The flame is small at first, but as the smell of smoke fills the air, so does the light from the fire. I will myself up and push past the pins and needles in my arms and legs. Then I draw myself toward the warmth.

It all hurts a little, the heat interacting with my frigid skin that's half asleep from the way I was lying, from the cold.

I shudder, and Jonah goes to my pack and pulls out a fluffy blanket.

"Look at you," he says, "all prepared."

I try to say, "That's my middle name," but it comes out garbled from my chattering teeth. I doubt he even knows what I was saying; I probably sound completely out of it. But I'm too exhausted and freezing to be embarrassed.

He drapes the blanket over my shoulders and I try, I *try* to focus on the warmth it provides. To will myself into existing like a human.

"Better?" he says.

"Sure," I lie.

"Why don't you have something to drink?"

I shake my head. "I've taken enough of our water."

"No," he says, "you haven't. Not if you're battling altitude sickness. You get dehydrated, you're only going to make things worse."

I roll my eyes. "I'm fine, Jonah."

His voice shifts so fast it makes my head spin. "No,

dumbass." I blink at him. "If you get sicker because you're trying to be noble, it's going to slow us both down tomorrow. Then I cover less ground. Then you get us both killed."

"O-oh," I say.

"Drink the water."

I swallow. My mouth is tacky, and forming the necessary saliva is an effort, so maybe he has a point.

I open one of the water bottles we brought and take slow sips.

"Happy now?" I say.

He shrugs and stares at the fire, then rips into a big hunk of beef jerky.

He's staring *so intently* away from me, so deeply disaffected by it all, that it almost circles around to *affected*. That's probably me wishfully thinking. Wishing I was stranded in the mountains with someone who gave a shit about me, not someone who's going to bully me into drinking water when I'm sick instead of gently, like, caressing my check and whispering that I need to take care of myself.

"Shit," he says when he bites off another chunk, "this tastes good."

Yeah. It was just me.

"The water," I admit, "does not suck."

I glance up at the sky again, the utter artwork of the sunset. A Colorado sunset has always been hard to beat, and in the isolated silence, trees cutting into it like they were drawn this way, it's pretty breathtaking.

Jonah draws closer to me and I tense.

He says, "Body heat."

I say, "If you're trying to get me naked right now . . ."

Jonah rolls his eyes. "Trust me, Jacob, if I wanted to get you naked, you'd know."

My face goes bright red and, for the first time this trip, I'm thankful for the cold that disguises the reason.

We sit in quiet as the sun dips below the horizon and the sky darkens.

I can't decide if the silence is unnerving or if it feels right.

It feels almost familiar after the full day of it.

But it feels . . . lonely, almost, too.

I get a pang, missing my cousins. Wishing I could use Jolie as a buffer, tease her about the girl she likes, get pelted in the face with a snowball by Jaxon and yell at him when there was a little too much ice razored through it.

"Do you think . . ." I start.

"Do I think what?"

"Do you think they're alright?"

Jonah doesn't answer right away. He measures his words when he's worried about honesty, I think.

"Yeah, Hallie. I think they're okay."

I blink at the fire and shift closer. To the flame, to Jonah. My blanket brushes his coat. "Do you think we were stupid to do this?"

"It doesn't matter," he says.

My breath shakes when I draw it into my lungs.

"You want any of this?" he asks me, wagging some trail mix in my face.

I instinctively jerk back and open my mouth to turn it down, and he says, "Oh wait. You're allergic to peanuts, right?"

I say, "Yup," then pause. "How did you know that?"

He furrows his brow. "I don't know if you know this, but we've kind of been doing these vacations for years."

"Yeah," I say. "But it's not like we've ever hung out."

"Not like we've ever been allowed to." There's a note of resentment in his voice that is so freaking pleasing.

"So how . . ."

"I pay attention," he says.

I glance over at him, but he's staring at the fire again. His arms are draped over his knees but his biceps are the littlest bit tense.

Tiny sparks flick off the flames, bright orange against white smoke.

It is a strange time, maybe, to think about anything but the cold. Anything but the dark.

But the fire itself is so . . . bizarrely comforting. Not just because it's warm.

Because it's fire. Because I'm a Jew.

I haven't practiced Judaism much at home in a long time; my parents haven't practiced in years and years, so it feels . . . awkward to, like, light candles on my own. But every trip we make to my cousins', I look forward to Shabbos, to Havdalah, like they're literal gifts. I feel the yearning in my blood, the desire for connection to a people, to my childhood, to . . . I couldn't even really say what. I'm Jewish no matter what I do. Whether I keep kosher or light candles or believe in G-d or don't.

I know that.

Judaism is a people and a culture and a religion and a thousand different things, and it's me, either way. But when I'm with them, it's not something I know. It something that—well, it *feels* like the people and the practice are mine.

So much of Jewish ritual is kindled in fire. It's in Havdalah, in Shabbos, in Rosh Hashanah and Yom Kippur and *Black fire on white fire* and day after day after holy day; I don't get to kindle flame for tradition, really, outside Uncle Reuben and Aunt Adah's, and every time I do, it's almost painful to acknowledge that I miss it—that I really *miss* something from when I was five years old.

Fire is so deeply a part of our tradition that looking at it, now, of all times, in the lonely, dangerous dark, feels like wrapping a six-thousand-year-old blanket around me.

I keep these thoughts to myself and curl deeper into them.

This is too deeply private, too deeply mine.

The fire cracks, pops, hisses as it consumes the dead things we fed it, and darkness falls.

In the dark, every noise feels louder.

The fact that we don't have a tent or a cave or any cover that isn't trees becomes so much more evident tonight—alone, in the dark.

Somewhere far off, or I hope it's far off, a howl slices through the quiet, and I shrink against Jonah. He casually slides an arm over my shoulder and pulls me into him, and it's so solid, so comforting, it doesn't even feel sexual.

It doesn't feel like A Move.

It feels necessary. It feels like human connection in the dark.

I can feel the strength in his arms, the solid rise of his chest when he hugs me close to him and rests his chin on my head.

It's too intimate, but it's not close enough.

"It's okay," he says.

"No, it's not," I say.

We might as well be strangers.

But he presses his mouth into my hair.

CHAPTER TWELVE

I AM AWAKE FOR the ninth time.

In the deep, fathomless dark.

Again when the stars have shifted in the sky.

One more time when the black turns to gray.

The sun rises and I lie there tucked against his chest, shuddering. He curls his arms around me and I push back into him because maybe I can get warm. Maybe I can trick my body into thinking this tiny increase in body temperature passes for heat.

Maybe the points of my spine that press into his chest will catch fire.

If I imagine it hard enough, I can pretend well enough that it's real.

I blow out through my mouth, and the moisture clouds on the gray-dark air.

His breath feathers my hair, warm on the back of my neck, and I can't even appreciate being this close to this cute a boy, can't really relish the musculature of his arms around me, the feel of his mouth so close to my skin.

All I can think of is the warmth, the most basic desire for temperature, for something that passes for shelter.

I can't stop thinking about how the air prickles my skin, how it seeps down through my big, fluffy coat to whisper over each little hair and bleed deep into my veins. And thinking about it makes me colder.

I shiver. Violently.

Jonah jumps and says, "What, what, what is—" Then his voice, rough with sleep, fades. I can feel him slow behind me. Stretching and groaning.

He says, "Sorry. You okay?"

"Mmhmm," I say.

He leans forward, just the smallest bit, and rests his forehead on the back of my neck. It prickles where his longish kinks and curls brush against me.

"We should get up," he mutters.

"But this ground is so comfortable."

I don't hear the laugh so much as I feel it.

He presses his fingertips, the smallest bits of pressure, into my shoulder, and I roll over to face him. My breath probably sucks. I don't think either of us cares.

He says, "How's that heart rate?"

I say, "Okay," and impossibly, given the situation in the most macrocosmic and microcosmic ways, I'm telling the truth.

"Your head?" He presses his knuckles to my forehead, which is no longer clammy.

"Yeah," I say. "I feel a lot better. Seriously."

He searches me for just a minute longer, then decides

to be satisfied. "Okay. Okay, you tell me if that changes today."

"Yeah," I say.

I snuggle back into him, like I can shut out the day looming ahead if I just use the large boy I barely know to keep me warm and safe.

"Come on," he says. He stands slowly. "Goddamn, my all of me."

"Ugh, oh no."

"Is this what it feels like to be thirty?"

I laugh, even though I know I'm about to be in a world of hurt. I curl up on myself just for a moment, to experience a half a second before reality sinks in, and then I stand.

"Fuck," I say. I wiggle my limbs and it comes out like this frantic dance. Half-growling, half-crying, trying to rid all my bones and muscles of the aftereffects of sleeping all night on the frozen ground.

"It's okay. Shake it off."

"I *am* shaking it off."

"Jesus, my back," he groans.

"Dude, *are* you thirty?"

He rolls his eyes and stretches up on his tiptoes, lengthening every muscle, reaching his fists to the sky in this wishbone of a position, and silhouetted against the blue-pink dark, he's fucking gorgeous.

My lips part watching him.

He settles back down on the balls of his feet and glances over at me, and I snap my mouth shut.

"Ready to get this party started?"

"Yeah," I say. I snag a small pack of Oreos out of his backpack and say, "Breakfast of champions."

He doesn't reach for his own bag of Oreos; he picks out of mine, and I know that's the right call. We need to conserve food. But my stomach twists when he does; I want to snarl and yank it back. The Oreos are the precious.

I don't. I keep a smile plastered on my face and watch while he consumes my calories.

"Let's formulate a plan," I say when the crunching subsides and we have both eaten enough to actually think.

"Well," he says, "that peak is out."

"Obviously."

"I mean . . . I don't really know if there's a plan to be had—"

"Downhill then," I say.

He purses his lips. "Why?"

"We can't go uphill."

"So that's it—that's the brilliant plot?"

I fold my arms across my chest. "Tell me if you've got something better."

"I don't. How could I? Your thing isn't exactly ironclad."

"But it's *something*."

He growls. "How about west?"

"West?" I say.

He points in the opposite direction of the sun. "Yes. West is back toward New Snowy Ridge."

I follow his finger and say, "That's where we were headed all day yesterday anyway. I say we keep an eye on the sun and work on heading downhill. We should find water."

"Hm," he says. "Well. You might have a point."

"I know."

"If we *can* find water, we can follow it down, at least to a drainage. Probably to a town or something."

I feel my posture straighten with pride. Look at me; I suggested something right. East Coast city girl *does* know something. Well, I mean, I knew the human body needed water to survive. That counts for . . . something.

I say, "I'm not arguing with you agreeing with me, but why does down equal town?"

"It doesn't exactly; it's just that that's where you're gonna find rivers. And people tend to have built up around rivers. Historically. Follow a river far enough, you'll stumble upon them eventually."

"Oh," I say. "Cool."

He starts walking, and I walk beside him, and when I see him out of the corner of my eye, he's hunched and tense. His expression has changed.

It changed the moment he said it.

I don't say what we're both thinking: how long is *eventually*? And how much *eventually* can we survive?

It's so quiet, for so long.

All I can hear is the quiet of the snowfall, the crunch of the snow under our feet.

The fear.

It should be quiet, a feeling like that. But it's not. It's all I can hear running through my head.

I think, as we walk, that it shouldn't be like this between

us. Quiet, odd. Jonah has never been exuberantly talkative. But it's not like . . . it's not like with Jaxon and Jolie, he's a man of few words. He's expressive and fun and witty and relaxed. Even with Tzipporah! With Sam!

It's not that he's just the strong, silent type.

It's that he's with me.

I chew my lip and run through the last seventeen years. I wonder what I've been kept from because my parents can't get their shit together.

I've been kept from a hundred Instagram conversations that I can't seem to break into, can't seem to understand, because I don't get my cousins' inside jokes.

From dances and talent shows and shopping and hiking and birthdays, because my parents decided to move to the other side of the country and to make sure everyone knew we were *separate* from all of them.

Some people have hard family, is the thing.

Some people have drama and toxicity and backstabbing.

They have people worth getting away from.

But I don't know. Walking with Jonah, I just . . . cannot stop thinking about the time I was twelve.

We were out here visiting, not for the annual ski trip for once, and I was at Jaxon and Jolie's house. They had no *idea* how hard I had to beg, to plead, to get my parents to let me go.

They had no idea that I watched my dad put on an eighty-dollar button-up and sixty-dollar tie to go to my Uncle Reuben's twelve-hundred-square-foot house, to tower over him in presence even though Uncle Reuben outweighs him by a good fifty pounds of muscle and fat.

They didn't know, and my dad didn't know, I could hear him through the door, because I was waiting, shrunken up against the plastic siding of the house, just below the window, instead of in the car where I should have been.

I'll never forget wanting to melt down into the mulch when my dad said, "Reuben, I swear to god, if my kid comes home smelling like weed after hanging out with *your* kid—"

"Jesus Christ, Uriah."

"No. I'm not being unreasonable here. I want her to have a good time with her cousins, but I know what they get up to."

"They're twelve and fourteen."

"And shouldn't be smoking weed and zipping all around the internet doing god knows what—"

"Oh please, like you weren't doing drugs and looking at porn when you were a teenager; I *lived* with you."

He lowered his voice and I didn't shrink; I rose up on my tiptoes to be able to hear better through the glass. "Just. Promise me none of this *I don't care if you drink as long as you do it my house* bullshit."

"She's bat mitzvah, Uri. You want me to give her grape juice tonight like a kid?"

"What?"

"It's Friday. It's Shabbat."

"Oh," he said. "Shabbat. Right. Right, well, I—well, that would. Be fine. But beyond that—"

"I fucking get it, man."

I remember my eyes going so wide I thought they'd pop out of my head. They stung with the force of it. It was the first time I'd ever heard a grown-up drop the f-bomb.

Uncle Reuben paused, and I could feel the silence like a stone. He said, "You've always been an asshole, but—" He lowered his voice so I really had to do my twelvest and strain to eavesdrop in the way only someone twelve and under can to hear the next part. "But you weren't this afraid for your *kid* until after I married Adah."

Dad was silent. Then he said, "Oh my *god*, Reuben. Is this . . . is this a race thing? You're saying I have a problem with you marrying a Black woman? You're calling me racist?"

Reuben said, "I'm just telling you what I'm seeing."

My whole body was hot. I didn't really want to think about that kind of thing being applied to my dad, but also . . . also I was sure Uncle Reuben and Aunt Adah had talked about it before now and probably they were . . . probably they were right. In some way.

I wrapped my arms around myself.

Just bury me in the ground.

There was the longest silence I'd experienced theretofore.

Then my dad said quietly, "I'll cover dinner for her. And your family if you could use—"

"Uriah. Just. Do you have somewhere to be?"

There were footsteps, and I scrambled to get out of the flower bed and up to the little stoop, because it wasn't like I'd saved myself enough time to sprint back to the car and throw myself through the windshield.

I'm sure I looked totally not at all suspicious when my dad opened the door and straightened that expensive, starched shirt, and said, "You need to call me to come pick you up, I'll be here in *ten minutes.*"

To Uncle Reuben's credit, his mouth was only pressed in a furious line for a half a second before he forced it into neutrality.

I was so freaking nervous, just absolutely sure we had ruined his night. Sure that he was going to be mad at me. That Aunt Adah was going to be upset.

I clutched my Poe Dameron backpack so hard that the texture of the straps left a pattern on my palm.

Then he said, "Hey, Hal," and smiled at me through the biggest, bushiest beard, like a brunette, Jewish Jeremiah Johnson. He'd always been so big and warm, and it was suddenly like my dad hadn't even been here telling him off.

I had loosened my grip and flung my arms around his solid middle, and he said, "Jaxon and Jolie are causing trouble inside, but don't tell your dad."

And I laughed and pushed past him into the house, wherein Jaxon and Jolie were most decidedly *not* causing trouble (until later). They were sitting around watching *Young Frankenstein* in the half-den downstairs, and when Jolie saw me coming down the three stairs that led to the room, she squealed and threw a pillow at me.

I bounced down and heard Jonah Ramirez's voice, yelling at Jolie, "Frau Blucher!"

And I froze.

If Dad knew . . .

But this movie was on and it smelled like popcorn and this house was a third the size of ours but I *loved* it and Jolie, Jolie above all. Jaxon was my next favorite . . . and honestly, Jonah was so deeply a unit with Jaxon that he was family, too.

Or something . . . something close enough.

Aunt Adah said, "Kids? Candle lighting in ten—get up here. I'm pulling challah out of the oven and your father is threatening to say hamotzi for every one of you and eat it all."

And of course.

Of course I stayed.

All that happened that night was we stayed up too late and played Truth or Dare.

And we all fell asleep in the den, and Aunt Adah woke me and Jolie and made us go to Jolie's room, because propriety.

And well. Dad found out that Jonah had stayed over.

I don't think I spent the night at my cousins' house again until I was sixteen.

At the time, I'd thought it was my fault.

I'd kind of blamed Jonah a little, too.

Now we're walking together, though, and I know . . . it wasn't me. It wasn't Jonah. It was my dad looking for an excuse to hate his brother.

A hundred miles away and years later, silent in the woods, it's still affecting us.

CHAPTER THIRTEEN

"SO. ALLERGIC TO PEANUTS," he says.

"Hmmm?"

"What else?"

I cock my head at him, mouth tipping up.

"Smoke."

He raises his eyebrow. "You shitting me? Don't you want to be a firefighter?"

"Cigarette smoke," I said. "But look at you, paying attention."

He shrugs. "Chick firefighter. It's kinda hot."

I groan, but I like it.

"That's sexist probably."

He says, "I don't know what to tell you."

"What else have you learned about me?"

He turns that knife of a smile on me and says, "You fishing, Jacob?"

"I'm trying to make conversation."

"Mmhmm. Well. You're into dance, right? Like ... something nerdy, I think. Ballroom?"

I blush. "Watching it, not doing it."

"That's even nerdier. And I know you've got a huge thing for Gene *Wilder*, you freak."

I laugh and shove his arm. "I don't have a thing for Gene Wilder."

"Yeah, you do."

He's right. I do.

I don't say anything and his face goes all smug, like he's not totally freezing and tired.

He says, "Okay, do me now."

I say, "Jonah, that's so forward."

"Christ." He laughs. Jagged edges and arrogance.

"You're an anthropology major."

"Easy."

"You love football." He gives me this unimpressed look and follows it up with a dismissive jack-off motion.

"Oh my god," I say. He takes a small swallow of his water and I say, "The steel guitar. You would die for the *steel guitar*."

He chokes. "Who told you that?"

"No one told me."

"Bullshit."

"Every time Uncle Reuben puts on bluegrass and the cousins make him turn it off, your eyes turn to little hearts. You're, like, romantically attracted to the steel guitar."

"I'm not romantically attracted to anyone, Jacob."

"Except the steel guitar."

"Christ, never tell anyone."

"Scout's honor," I say.

"You're not a scout."

"But I'm honorable."

It can't be intentional when he bumps my shoulder and says, "Bet you're not *that* honorable."

I scrape my teeth over my lip, but he's not looking at me anymore; he's moving ahead, into the wild.

Every foot we descend, it's like I can feel the air seeping back into my lungs, so I don't complain.

Even though the air's still thin and my legs hurt and I'm exhausted.

"You are, though."

He laughs. "Honorable?"

"A scout."

He spins around to face me, takes two steps backward to pop me the nerdy-ass Boy Scout salute, and completes the rotation so he's facing forward again.

"How the hell does that work?" I say.

"What? Scouting?"

"I don't know." I shrug. "Just . . . someone like you. In the Boy Scouts."

He looks over his shoulder at me and slows a tic so I can catch up. He clutches his hand to his chest. "Jacob, that hurts. What are you skeptical of? My reluctance to wear a uniform or my ability to tie knots?"

I swallow hard. "Uniform. And like. G-d and country and all of that."

He says, "Well thank fuck. I can tie knots like a pro. And I don't know, fuck patriotism, but I like being around everyone. I like being in the woods."

"Mm," I say.

"Hate that uniform, though."

I grin.

"You think I don't believe in G-d?"

"No," I say. "I didn't say that. Scouts just seems like a lot."

"I believe in G-d."

"Yeah?"

"Not like glory hallelujah and stuff, I guess. But. Yeah."

"Tell me."

"What I believe about G-d?"

I shrug. "Yeah."

"You interested in that, really?"

I furrow my brow. "Why wouldn't I be?"

He chews on it for a second, micro-expressions moving over his face in the most fascinating way. "Just—huh, I don't know. Girls don't usually get me alone and ask me about theology."

"Mm, a little occupied, typically?"

He smirks. "Something like that."

"Well," I say, "we're not. We've got a whole lot of mountain and even more silence."

He runs his tongue over his teeth. "I don't want to, like, offend you or whatever."

"Offend me?"

He purses his lips and shoves his hands down deep in his pocket. "You're religious and shit. I don't want to piss you off."

I bark out a laugh. "I'm sorry, I think you're confusing me with a Not A Jew."

He raises an eyebrow.

"It's not like you have to believe in G-d to be a Jew."

He furrows his brow. "What?"

"A Jew is a Jew, dude. I could be an atheist or a theist or

keep kosher or eat nothing at all but pork and bacon every day, and when I died of scurvy, I'd die a Jew. I can do tzedakah all day every day and then light candles on Shabbos and still decide I wanna play video games, and I'm still a freaking Jew. An observant one. Or a non-observant one. Whatever."

"That's . . ." He scratches the back of his head. "Huh."

"You never talked to Jaxon about this? Oh, sorry—*Jax*."

He grins and flips me off, then says, "Nah. We don't talk about religion a whole lot. I know he cares about it. But that's about as far as we get."

"Well," I say, shuddering against a quick, cold breeze, "trust me; whatever you have to say, I've probably heard it and eighty other opinions from a million rabbis and whatever you think just . . . could not possibly offend me. Not the way it works."

"Oh." He takes a minute to squint up at the sky and just generally be awkward. Then he says, "I uh, I don't know. I guess I think G-d was probably there once. And now He's—She's? They're—G-d was probably there once and now probably G-d's got other shit to do."

"You think?" I say. If I keep talking, I won't think about the sharp pain in my stomach and weakness in my legs that are begging me to eat. "G-d exists but forgot about everyone?"

He shrugs. "Probably intentional. That's what I'd do. Just go the fuck away, wash my hands of it."

"You're not G-d, though."

"I'm just saying, if I made a diorama and it came to life, and then a bajillion years later, I decided to fill it with little dudes who, in the span of five minutes, managed to totally wreck each other and burn down the whole diorama and fuck over everything else I'd put in it, I'd just throw my hands up and leave them to deal with it. That's exhausting."

"That seems . . ." I glance up at the sky. "Lonely."

"Yeah?"

"Yeah." I twist my hands in my pockets. "Like if someone intentionally put us here, for a reason, and then left? That feels . . . so abandoned."

"Never said G-d made people for a reason. What if G-d was just bullshitting, you know? And we all went wrong?"

"That's bleak."

"It's not bleak; it's reality. Look at us. Look at everyone. Look at what we did, what we do. If there's a purpose, I bet we fucked it up."

"Mmm," I say. "No. No, I don't—I don't think so."

"Well," he says, shoving his hands down in his pockets. His mouth curls up like he's comfortable, but I can see his jaw clench and lock, can see him shivering, even with the coat. The bright sky has shifted just a little gray while we've walked, and I can feel the temperature drop. Just exactly what we needed. He glances up at it, then back forward, to the non-path we're creating in the snow. "Enlighten me."

I say, through my chattering teeth, "I just don't think there's like, no point to any of it. I don't think G-d made people and we went haywire."

He raises an eyebrow. "Ice caps are melting, everyone's shooting each other and bombing each other, everyone's killing each other and caging each other because they were born on the wrong side of a border. You don't call that haywire?"

I shrug, or try. It might be that my shoulders are so stiff, that my blood is so thick and cold, that my arms don't actually move and I just project a shrug. "It's bad. It's messed up, I guess. I know. But I just . . . I guess I think that when it comes down to it, it's not my job to figure out if the whole world's fucked; it's my job to try to make it better."

He nudges my arm. "Think you can save the world, huh?"

"No." I shake my head because that's not what I mean, and suddenly this conversation seems like the most important thing in the world. Maybe because it's so quiet around us, so empty. Like we're living in a vacuum, like we're having a conversation in space. Any words get swallowed up the second either of us says them and all that matters is listening until they do. I press my hand into his arm over his coat, curl my fingers, and he stops. I say, "I don't want to save the world. I just—I want to make it the tiniest bit better. And that's enough."

It's tikkun olam, repairing the world, and it's not like I've talked about this with my friends. No one wants to sit down and discuss religion, really, and we don't go to temple much anymore. Mom and Dad stopped having time when I was a kid, when we moved to Massachusetts. But I picked up this much.

And voicing it makes it feel a little like it's mine.

I catch Jonah blinking down at me, not looking above it all, not looking sarcastic for once. His eyes are bright and open and focused.

Just . . . a little lit up.

The tiniest spark of fire.

It doesn't matter if I blush; I know my nose and cheeks and chin are so red already.

He says, "Is that why you want to be a firefighter?"

"Yeah," I say. "Yeah, I guess so."

"You guess so?"

"I'm into the idea of public service."

"Of course you are," he says. "Goody two-shoes."

I roll my eyes. "But I'm not a teacher, I'm definitely not a politician."

"Not a cop?" he says.

"Oh Jesus, no," I say.

"You sure?"

"All cops are bastards, Jonah."

He actually cackles. It doesn't mute like I think it should. The endless space doesn't swallow it whole. It echoes.

Then it's nothing but quiet and snowfall.

I say, "I like the idea of pulling people from burning buildings. I like the physicality. I like the challenge."

"Mmm."

"And I have a plan."

"Well, hit me with it."

I say, "I've already taken most of my first year of classes. Just another semester and I can be an EMT. Then I can get paramedic certification. If I apply when I'm eighteen, it shouldn't take too long to get on with the city. I mean, sometimes it does. Everyone wants to be a firefighter from the time they're six."

"Did you?" he says.

"When I was six? I wanted to be a unicorn."

That laugh again—that warms me up every time I hear it, every time I'm the one to make it happen, even though I'm sure he's laughed like that for a lot of girls.

I'm sure it doesn't make me special; it just makes me the girl he's trapped on a mountain with.

Still, I'll take whatever warmth I can get.

"Anyway," I say, spine straight now that I'm talking about this, this area I'm in control of, that I'm comfortable with. That I've laid out in careful block print since I was fourteen years old. "So anyway, it could take a while, especially in Boston. But if I jump in with my paramedic cert already, that should help. I'll wait it out in an ambulance until then, gain experience until I can do what I really want."

"You're going back to Boston?"

"Yeah," I say, and bitterness I didn't intend to express creeps into my voice. "Of course. That's the plan. That's always been the plan."

"You really get off on plans, don't you, Jacob?"

I furrow my brow. "I don't think I'd phrase it that way."

"Oh, too crass for your delicate ears?"

"Shut up."

"You really *take pleasure* in plans, don't you?"

"Jesus, dude, that's worse."

He laughs.

"I'm not that obsessed with plans."

"HA. Okay."

"Well, what about you, Mr. Devil May Care? I bet you have college mapped out. I bet you *get off on it*."

His eyes brighten again and I can feel it down to my

toes this time. "No, nerd. I don't *get off* on college, but yeah, I'd sure as hell *better* have a map. I'm a sophomore."

"Right," I say. I don't know why I'd forgotten that. He's two years older than I am. He both seems totally experienced like that *and* totally like he's still in high school. Like he's my age. I don't know, it's hard to parse out and harder to explain.

"I'm on track. I've switched majors three times, but I got my gen eds first. I'm actually double majoring. Not just in anthro. Finally getting into what I care about."

"And what's that?"

"Poli sci."

"Seriously?" I say, blinking. I don't know why that's a surprise. Honestly, I don't know what he could have said that *wouldn't* have been surprising.

"Yeah, seriously. I don't know what I want to do with it yet. Maybe international relations. Maybe I want to get more into activism, really fuck up all the Nazis in Denver, you know?"

"Yeah," I say, even though I don't know. Not really.

Normally, I'd let that slide. Pretend I knew more than I did and google it, but suddenly I feel naked. Without my smartphone, without access to the knowledge of the whole world at my fingertips.

And I feel like . . . like for once, pretending is wasting time.

I blink at the snowy ground in front of me, realizing just now that my toes have gone numb. That . . . can't be good.

But it's not like there's anywhere good to stop.

Not like there's anything here but more snow, more snow, more snow.

So I say—even though asking a question of another human being, a question I could have found the answer to myself under normal circumstances, feels shockingly, startlingly vulnerable—"I didn't . . . I thought Denver was, like, this liberal paradise."

It's silent for a second, and then Jonah laughs out loud. "Yeah, you want progressive, let me just point you at a city with a fuck-ton of white people in it."

"Oh," I say. "Huh. Yeah, good point."

Jonah runs a hand back over his hair. He wears it big and natural, and the snow dots it with little white freckles before it melts. His fingers are chapped already—they're flaking and a little pale. I don't even want to know what mine look like. They're probably cracked. Thankfully, they're under the gloves that halfway dried overnight. If I see them bleeding, it will only make it worse.

"Let me just . . . let me put it this way. Denver votes blue. It's liberal. It's *liberal*. It's not *progressive*. Denver votes to let people do whatever the hell they want to do, so they can shut up about it and live their lives and not worry about you after election day."

I don't say anything. I wait. I walk. I don't want to say a thing because, for the first time, maybe in forever, I'm listening to Jonah be passionate about something. Getting a glimpse into what he really cares about, what he's majoring in, something beyond him bullshitting tough and hitting on me.

I *listen*.

He says, "Because they vote for Democrats and whatever the fuck. And then the city passes legislation that bans homeless people from sleeping in public, and no one but a couple activists cares. They vote to let people smoke weed, but let every Black dude who's been locked up for weed in the city stay locked away in jail for shit white people can do legally now. They fake like they're progressive and then write up profiles on Nazis like what matters is their haircuts. Do you even fucking *know* how many Nazis there are here?"

I swallow. "I should, I guess. Nazis all over in Massachusetts too and, like, welcome to Whiteville. I've gone to protests and seen my cemeteries vandalized. I know about Nazis, man."

He says, "Yeah. I guess you would, huh."

I shrug. "Comes with the Tribe. But I don't know. I guess I didn't think it would be worse here than a million other places."

"It's just that—no one cares here. No one cares. Even though all the Denver patriot militias are taking over the goddamn city. Because *that* would require getting up off their asses and caring about people who aren't rich and straight and abled and white. That would require being impolite. It would require not being Apathy, the City™. Anyway," he says, clearing his throat. "Sorry, yeah, anyway. It just gets me so furious that people think Portland and Seattle and Denver are the least racist places in the country, like it's even physically possible for totally white-ass places to somehow be the *least racist*. Jesus. Anyway. Anyway. Poli sci." Another clearing of the throat. "I'm kind of . . . I kind of get a little overly passionate. Or whatever."

Now I bet my eyes look like a She-Ra character's. All sparkles and sunshine. Like his did a second ago. Because my gosh, I've never seen him . . . never seen him care. Like this. Enough to get lost in his own head yelling about something.

It's not what I ever expected of him.

I guess that's not fair, because how can either of us really know enough about the other to have any expectations?

But here I am.

Surprised.

I say, "No. It's good. To care."

He shrugs.

"Especially when it's something like that. That matters."

He just kind of grunts and keeps walking.

And the snow continues to fall.

CHAPTER FOURTEEN

WHEN THE SKY CLEARS and the exhaustion sets in, we find a copse of trees to sink into and eat lunch.

Lunch is a total feast: granola! Jerky! Some cheese. I feel a little weird eating the beef and cheese together because it's not kosher, and even though my parents don't keep it anymore, that's something I never felt right about. There's a lot of mitzvot I don't keep, like, a *lot*, but the kashrut stuff was too drilled into me as a little kid, I think, living near my grandparents out here. So yeah, I feel weird. Weird enough to hesitate. But preservation of life is like, NUMBER ONE and supersedes almost *everything* when it comes down to it, so that matters a whole lot more than not eating milk and meat together. This feels *pretty* preservation-of-lifey, so I tear into both.

My stomach hurts.

I twist open the last water bottle in our bag and take a long drink. "Fuck," I whisper.

Jonah glances at it grimly and takes a swallow, Adam's apple shifting with the effort.

His eyes linger on the water level.

I follow his gaze and say, "We could just . . . we're surrounded by snow, right?"

"Yeah," he says. "But it's—we can't just eat it."

"Why not?" It comes out defensive, angry almost. I blink at myself. "Right. Sorry. Right, the hypothermia. We'll die." I don't say anything else. I just take another swallow, smaller this time. Less than I want to. Less than my throat is begging me for.

Neither of us speaks for a minute, and I wonder if he's thinking what I'm thinking: that neither of us had said that word yet: *die.*

And suddenly it's a real possibility.

After taking a moment to breathe, I glance up at him and offer him the bottle.

His pupils dilate right in front of me, looking at it.

We used to play a game like that back in middle school, back when one of us learned that your pupils dilate when you look at something you want. We'd say the name of someone cute and watch everyone's eyes. Or, if someone didn't know about the science, we'd troll him by having him look at whoever it was we wanted to know about.

Of course, we'd always just accuse whoever we *wanted* of the appropriate level of pupil dilation, because like that would have ever actually worked. Like we could have actually *seen* the tiny physical response like that with the naked eye.

The point is, this time, I see it.

He shakes his head and stands, shaking his hands out.

"Get up," he says.

"Excuse me?"

"Get up."

I scoff at being told what to do but ultimately stand like he says to.

He's moving from foot to foot, and I don't know how he has the energy but I guess he does. Probably the burst from that whole ninety calories coursing through him.

"It'll warm you up, man—move."

"I'm tired," I say.

He rolls his eyes and says, "Christ, you whiner."

I rub my hands together and hop in place to get my blood moving. "You're an asshole."

He smiles, baring his teeth.

"Now listen," he says. "I told you I was gonna teach you some mountain lion protection techniques."

"Ah right, yes. Lest a wild animal attack us." I say that like it's not a real possibility, like this whole thing is fake and I'm watching it on a screen.

"Yeeeessss," he says. "There's animals here; it's the woods."

I narrow my eyes. "Thanks, did the Boy Scouts teach you that?"

He flips his middle finger at me and says, "Listen, smartass."

"Mmhmm."

"A mountain lion comes at you, you're gonna want to run. Don't do that."

"O-okay."

"You want to start by looking tough. Which . . . good luck."

I groan and close the distance between us to shove him.

He stumbles back on his heels and laughs. "Make yourself big and back up."

"I thought you said earlier that I should stand my ground?"

"Yeah, but you stand still, you get eaten. You run, you get eaten."

"Not leaving me with a whole lot of options here, slick."

"Be big. Back slowly away."

I blow out a breath. "Bigger than a mountain lion?"

"Yeah," he says. "You're probably bigger than a lion, dude."

"What?"

"I was on a hunt a couple years back and the guy bagged a really big cat. Just short of the books. You know how big he was? Like a buck fifty."

Oh. Well. Alright then.

I entallen myself. I hold my arms so that it really looks like I have biceps. I *do* have biceps, as a matter of fact; you want to be a firefighter, you lift heavy. But I exaggerate the stance. I puff out my chest.

Jonah smiles. "Nice. So you back off. Slow. And you yell. Huge, loud noises. Make yourself totally terrifying. Hopefully he doesn't touch you."

I nod. It's still a game when we're playing it this way, still not real. It's dress rehearsal, not the show.

"What happens if he attacks anyway?"

Jonah chews on the inside of his cheek.

"I'm dead?" I take that to mean.

"Not necessarily. You hear about that dude who got attacked by a lion while he was out running in Colorado? Choked the thing out?"

"Holy shit," I say.

"Yeah. *Someone's* never hurting for a blow job again."

I snort.

"Priority," he says, "is to protect yourself."

"Duh."

He takes a step closer to me, and a cold breeze whispers its way into my coat, a couple errant snowflakes riding on it. It's not even really snowing; it's just like the world is existing in the middle of a floating drift. Lazy flakes deciding to form here and there and melt any place your skin had started to acclimate.

"So," he says, "a lion attacks you, he's going to go for your neck. Protect it. No matter what."

My own hand instinctively slips up toward my throat, and he says, "No. Like this," and grabs my wrist, then yanks it away from my jugular. He takes my left wrist in his other hand, and god, his hands are so *big* that he can loop his index finger all the way around my bones until it overlaps his whole thumb. I swallow hard as he presses into my pulse and shoves my hands so they're around the back of my neck, elbows coming together in front of my throat.

"Like this," he says.

His chest is pressed against mine, and I can feel him shift, even under the coat. I can see the pulse pounding in the veins of his throat, make out every little hair on his face that he hasn't shaved in days.

My pulse is jumping all over the place; I can't breathe.

"You got it?" he says, staring down at me.

I'm so cold, and I'm so tired, and I'm so . . . I can't stop looking at his mouth.

He is breathing my air.

I watch his breath cloud out into the cold and disappear when I inhale.

"I—yeah," I say.

He drops my hands and I only have a heartbeat to recover before he's backing up and crouching, circling like he's going to attack me.

My eyebrows shoot up to my hairline and he lunges.

I forget everything.

I forget what to protect, I forget my hand placement, I forget.

Until he's chest to chest with me again, huge hand digging into the back of my neck like jaws.

"Game over," he whispers.

I fucking shudder.

He doesn't let go.

I can't stop looking at him, can't stop breathing in the cool scent of the mountain snow combined with sweat, can't tell the difference between the adrenaline running because of potential mountain lion attack versus the intolerable closeness of Jonah freaking Ramirez. I am *overwhelmed.*

The points of his fingertips are digging into the muscles of my neck.

They're going to bruise.

He says, voice low, "Protect yourself."

I shake him off and back up.

If just . . . to be able to breathe, *Jesus.*

He cocks his head. "You ready?"

I open my mouth to say yes and he comes at me, and

this time, I bring my arms up around my neck, elbows at my throat.

He grabs for my arm and I shove him off.

He comes at my back, and I whirl around in time for him to grab at my neck again. But my arms are in the way.

He clamps down on my forearm and spins me so my back is pressed to his chest.

"Not bad," he says into my ear.

I feel myself lean, relaxing back into him.

I feel him breathe.

I feel him smile against my ear.

And I elbow him in the stomach.

"Fuck, goddamn, shit—"

He coughs and I prance forward. "Protect yourself."

I face him, hand on my hip, and he's doubled over, breathing.

After a minute, in which I am only slightly concerned that I took it too far, he pushes up with his hands on his knees.

Then he manages to stand.

He coughs out a laugh.

"Well," he says, "lesson learned."

"You think I can survive a cougar?"

He shrugs. "Beats me, but I'm sure as hell not going through another drill."

I laugh and he breathes jaggedly for another minute before glancing up at the sky that's going gray.

"Come on," he says. "We should keeping moving."

Yeah.

Yeah, I guess we should.

CHAPTER FIFTEEN

THE PRIORITY, WE HAVE decided, has to be finding water, and not just water but *drinking* water. It wasn't something either of us thought of earlier even though it should have been; it should have been the very first thing. Because when you're surrounded by water, even if it's in the wrong form, it's so easy to forget that you might die.

I guess the priority was water to begin with: rivers leading to civilization and all that. But now it's urgent.

Now that our water bottles are gone, it's necessary.

We've both filled our water bottles with snow and keep shaking them and wrapping them in our coats and breathing on them and doing whatever we can to get them to melt into something drinkable, something that won't make either of us freeze to death.

We've been walking all day and at least we seem to be descending, when it comes to altitude, which? I guess is good? But I feel like we're getting nowhere.

I feel like we're complete idiots.

How many stories have both of us read of hikers who

left the vehicle and died in the desert, you know? This is like Getting Lost 101—you don't do this.

But I keep thinking about Sam.

I keep thinking about Lydia

Someone had to do *something* for them, right?

They had to—they had to.

I hug my arms around me as my breath clouds and my lips actually *feel* blue.

If I tell myself this was the right decision over and over, it will somehow change things. Like the principle of the matter will save my life.

Our lives.

I watch Jonah, trudging along, hands shoved deep down into his pockets, head down, and see him shiver.

For some reason, that's so fucking terrifying.

Like that really confirms it's cold.

I wonder how everyone is, and then I shut my eyes tight and block it out. I can't think about that—they're fine. Everyone is fine, and we have to press on like they're okay, and we are their last hope.

The sun falls fast when it falls.

The sky goes from light to dark in a heartbeat; it's almost eerie.

But there's nowhere to sleep and we both know it. We can't hunker down until we find something that doesn't mean lying on the snow under a pine tree again. I don't know about Jonah, but my significantly in-shape muscles are screaming and my back is screaming and the idea of shivering on the ground with the complete lack of cover we have right now, just us and the coyotes howling, makes me want to die.

I can't.

We can't.

Neither of us says anything.

We just both understand—and keep walking.

Eventually, trees appear again, yay hooray.

The night gets darker and colder and, I swear to god, I'm about to just start crying and I probably already would have if I wasn't so deeply conscientious of keeping all possible water inside me right now.

Jonah says, "Hal," and looks back at me.

I take a deep breath. We have to stop eventually.

But *god*, another night on the forest floor.

I don't know what about the dark makes everything stand out so starkly—the cold, the loneliness, the panic.

"Hallie," says Jonah.

He can sense it, I guess. Or it's written totally plainly on my face.

It doesn't matter. I'm shaking. I'm just *cold* and I'm just—I'm *scared.*

Jonah crosses the couple of steps it takes to close the gap between us and says, "Hey, look up."

I do. There's nothing.

He says, "You see that constellation?"

I frown. "What constellation?"

"Up there?" I follow his finger. "It's called Orion."

I roll my eyes. "Thanks, yes, I know what Orion looks like—"

"Well, we only say that now because they used to call him *Old Ryan.*"

I pause. I stand up a little straighter. "I'm sorry, what?"

"Old Ryan. He was a hunter."

Okay, well that part is true, so now I'm really not sure where he's coming from.

"He had two brothers: Young Ryan and Medium Ryan. And one day they were all out hunting—"

"Jonah, you expect me to believe that Orion—"

"Old Ryan, please give him the proper respect."

I cross my arms over my chest and blow out an exasperated breath through my nose. "You expect me to believe that Orion had two little brothers who were named, IN THE ANCIENT GREEK, YOUNG RYAN. And MEDIUM RYAN."

"Thank you for paying attention; the class is all impressed at your display of knowledge. Now. Let me continue."

I throw my hands in the air.

Jonah looks up at the sky. "Now, one day, the three brothers went hunting in the woods. As you can see around Old Ryan up there."

"There's no woods around Old Ryan. Orion. Oh my god."

His eyes start to sparkle. "Young Ryan had gotten jealous of Old Ryan's treatment as a hero even though Old Ryan was a fool with nothing special about him but a magical bow that only he could lift. But Young Ryan was a shapeshifter. A Trickster."

"This—is this Loki? Are you talking about Thor and Loki—"

"So he and Medium Ryan conspired against him, because he was bound by a vow never to harm either of his brothers."

"Who bound him?"

"Well that's kind of a personal question, don't you think?"

I stare at him, nonplussed.

He raises a brow and says, "A witch."

"What's her name?"

"Witch."

"Jesus."

"Now you're being weird about it. So Medium Ryan runs off with Old Ryan into the woods. and even though they're looking for more traditional game, Young Ryan turns into a monstrously huge water bird. And he flaps in front of them, glowing and majestic, an absolute *trophy*. Old Ryan is overcome and shoots at his brother. Medium Ryan, of course, misdirects the arrow, so it only nicks him, but that's enough."

"How?" I say.

"How what?"

"How does he misdirect it?"

"Magic."

"From what?"

Jonah looks down his nose at me and says, "The witch."

"Oh my god. Jonah."

"Who *shows up* the moment he draws blood. Old Ryan is very sad, of course, utterly repentant, but the witch and her magic care not. He has broken his vow and now must be cast off the earth into the sky."

"The end. Thank god."

"And that," says Jonah, "is where we get the phrase, *Shoot for the loon. Even if you miss, you'll still become a bunch of stars.*"

"*Jonah*," I groan. I grab his arms and I actually shake him. "That whole thing? Was that whole thing for a punch line?"

"It was to impart knowledge to you; I'm trying to help you."

"It's bullshit!"

"It's not bullshit," he says. "It's all true."

His mouth is turned up and then he's laughing and I'm laughing and . . . and I can't even be mad because for two minutes, I forgot I was terrified.

And now I'm not shaking and ready to bury myself in the ground.

I shut my eyes.

Reorient.

I'm prepared to find a place. To sleep. On the cold ground. Again.

I blow out a breath, open my eyes, then they widen. "Wait," I say.

He furrows his brow. "What?"

"Oh god. Yes. There. *Look*." For the first time in hours, I have *energy*. YES. I point several yards away and he follows my finger to what I am 99 percent sure is a hunting blind.

CHAPTER SIXTEEN

"OH MY *GOD*," HE says, and I swear it sounds almost sexual.

"Thank fuck," I say. "Thank fuck for hunters, oh my god oh my god."

Jonah powers toward the structure so fast that he's moving at just this side of a run, and so am I. We reach the base of the tree and I shake out my hands to release the nervous energy, which is pretty stupid, I guess—conserving energy is the thing to do right now. But it's instinct. I'm so freaking excited.

The blind is constructed in a tree, and there are haphazard steps nailed up the trunk. They lead to a box big enough for a person and a half, but the important thing is that it's wooden and it's enclosed, and the only windows are closed up with a tarp.

Oh my *gosh*, it's like a five-star hotel.

I clasp one of the steps and that's it, now I'm crying.

Jonah says, "Pull it together, man."

"I can't."

"I know," he says. "Goddamn, it's beautiful."

I pull myself up the treehouse ladder step by step. It wasn't clear to me until this moment just how weak I'd gotten over the last couple days, but thank god I lift heavy. Thank god I've been training to firefight for two years and these guns absolutely do not lie.

Because those, even weakened, are what allow me to make it to the top.

Jonah is struggling just a little, and he scoffs at first when I offer him a hand to pull him into the place, but not for so long that he doesn't eventually suck it up and accept my help.

We hoist him into the blind and he shuts the door behind him.

The instant temperature change is *incredible*. It's just a couple degrees, probably, but it means everything.

"Jesus," he says, "you're absolutely jacked."

I grin and strip off my coat, because it's way too close in here for us to both be done up like marshmallows, and the shield the wood provides has raised the temperature so much that I'm actually surprised that I'm a little uncomfortable.

I'm sure I won't be in a minute.

But I do strip off my coat, and then I flex.

Jonah rolls his eyes, but he's smiling.

"Impressive," he says.

"Oh, I know."

"And cocky."

I shrug, lit up from the discovery, and the compliment, and . . . and the fact that we are two not-entirely-small people in a blind built for a person and a half.

I sink to the floor and Jonah sinks with me, but we can't do that without tangling our legs together.

I try not to look at his face, to keep from acknowledging that my thighs are draped over his, that every time he shifts his foot, his shin brushes my calf.

"So, okay," he says. "I'm not—trying to be weird about this, but I'm going to take off my coat."

I do look at him then. "Join the club," I say. Mine is balled up behind me, giving me something to lean up against.

"Yeah," he says. He laughs and it's nervous. He sheds his coat, bumping my chest with his arms and who knows what other parts of him on the way out of it. Then he sets it behind him like I've done and shudders.

With both of us out of our massive layers, suddenly it seems so clear, so overwhelming how close we are to each other in this dark little box.

There is a wall at my back and side, and only a couple inches between my left and the door.

Jonah has even less space.

I can't move without every surface of my leg running over his calves, his torso, his thighs.

I blow out a breath and grab for the backpack I brought, shoved uncomfortably into the corner of the blind. I have a toothbrush, and I just yank it out of the bag with no fanfare, for something to do with my hands.

I brush my teeth, right there in the blind, like an absolute weirdo.

Then I open the door and spit.

Jonah looks at me like I'm a complete freak and says, "Are you serious?"

I shrug. "If no one thought that bringing a toothbrush to an event where drinking was going to occur, to freshen breath before going home to our parents, that's their fault."

He snorts. "You're something."

"Do you . . . want to use it?"

He wrinkles his nose. "Your toothbrush? I'm good. Give me some of that toothpaste, though, I guess."

He wets a little corner of a blanket in some snow that's stuck to the outside of the blind, squeezes on some toothpaste, and scours his teeth with the fabric. Then he spits out the door.

It's a flash of freezing cold, then warmth again, and we are left with quiet.

"Shit, that's so much better," he says.

And then we are here with nothing to do but breathe and acknowledge the absolute lack of space between us.

The dark, which makes it hard to see your hand in front of your face, let alone the other person. Makes everything feel even closer.

He shifts on his butt and his leg runs over mine.

I swallow hard, breathing in the scent of mint and old wood and the clean fury of the snow outside.

Jonah runs his thumb over his lower lip and says, quiet, "Again, not trying to be weird."

I raise an eyebrow, hoping that masks the nerves, the height in my pulse, the quick shallowness in my breathing.

"But you should like . . . shove up against me. I'm not trying to come onto you; it's just that—"

My stomach swoops and twists. I don't know if I'm relieved he's not *trying to come onto me* or disappointed, and that's so confusing that I don't even want to begin to deal with it, so I just cut him off and slide over to him. My knees press into his thighs and I turn around and lean so my back pushes into his chest, and I am sitting between his legs.

He blows out a shaky breath.

It's . . . well, it's cold. Of course he's shaking a little.

He pulls his legs in tight to me so that his inner thighs overtake my outer thighs, and his arms curl around my chest.

My head relaxes against the curve of his throat and I can feel his heart beat into my back.

Fuck.

Fuck.

Nature, I did not order this. I ordered two hunting blinds, there seems to have been a mistake; this forest only has one.

He exhales and it lifts the hairs on the top of my head.

I don't just hear it when he clears his throat; I *feel* it.

"Wish we had a fire," I say. I whisper it. Talking feels too loud.

He moves his jaw, but I don't know what his face looks like. I just feel the hard slant against my head. He moves, and something rustles, and the entire expanse of his chest draws fire over my back. That's one way to do it.

He comes back out of the bag he was evidently rummaging in with a little candle, and lights it with the lighter he keeps in his back pocket after pulling it a full five times.

"Cool," he says, late night scratch in his voice. "It would be good if the lighter I'd brought hadn't been fucking empty."

I actually laugh.

At a certain point, every absurd problem becomes legitimately funny.

As long as you don't think about it too hard.

Jonah pulls me in closer to him, and I grab my big, fluffy blanket from the other side of the blind to drape over us.

I can feel his muscles relax—strand by strand.

"You're gonna be so grounded after this," he whispers into my hair.

My pulse jumps so hard that there's no way he doesn't feel it.

"Can you imagine?" I say. "My dad will lose his shit."

"No prom for you."

"Not now." I shift, lean a little farther back so my hair falls over his shoulder and he sucks in a breath.

I feel his heartbeat speed against my spine.

"Why—" he starts, then abruptly stops.

I wait, trying to decide if I can let it go.

I can't.

There's nothing, nothing to distract myself. I say, "Why what?"

"Why do you guys hate me so much?"

I furrow my brow and turn my face, forgetting just how close we are, not realizing that that move will put my mouth a literal breath away from his throat. Just a centimeter from brushing his jaw. "I don't hate you."

He makes this noise that's caught between a choke and a laugh.

"I swear," I say.

"Your parents hate me."

"Well."

"Mmmhmm," he hums against my jaw.

"In fairness, my parents hate, like, everybody."

"*You*," he says, "are just afraid of me."

I frown. "What?" And whip my head so that I'm staring at him, even though it puts us in absolutely uncomfortable proximity. Even though it forces me to consciously still so that I don't shift and brush his mouth with mine.

. . . Thank god for toothpaste.

"Come on," he says, fingers slipping around my wrist, thumb pressing into my pulse. "It's like a rabbit's."

"No it isn't."

"Why do I freak you out, Hallie?"

"You don't."

He blinks, and I suddenly realize how long his eyelashes are.

His jaw is a little tight, mouth a disbelieving line. He's not mad, he just . . . thinks I'm full of shit.

I say, "I'm more afraid of my parents than I am of you."

"Well, no shit." He laughs and his breath is warm on my mouth.

And because it's easier not to look at him, because it's easier not to feel his laughter on my lips and watch his eyes react to everything I say, I turn again and lean back into his chest.

There is so much more of us pressed against each other this way, but it's not so intimate that I can't breathe.

The wind whistles through the slight imperfections in the wood the hunter used to put this blind together.

I shut my eyes, even in the dark. "It was easy to be just a little afraid of you."

He doesn't answer.

He breathes.

"As if you don't *want* people to be afraid of you."

The tiniest hum in his chest. It's almost an acknowledgment, but it stops just short.

I say, "You and Jaxon are so just—so wild, you know? And I only see you for fifteen seconds at a time and it's always one or both of you getting yelled at and one or both of you giving the middle finger to whatever authority figure has you nailed that time. I've heard the stories, dude."

He practically harrumphs. "What stories?"

"Lighting up in the principal's RV?"

He laughs out loud, raspy in my ear. "Oh shit, I'd forgotten about that."

"You're both getting into fights like every other week—"

"I've gotten into *two* fights. Jaxon's the Rocky Balboa here, not me. I might have let those rumors run, but in reality? The two fights I've gotten into, *his* scrawny ass *got* me into—what do you want me to do? Just let him get it handed to him because he couldn't keep his head down when a couple fucks decided they weren't going to leave him alone?"

"Hm," I say. That's . . . different than the impression I'd gotten.

"Didn't you punch a cop?"

He literally snorts, then shoves me just a little and presses his fingers into my shoulder so I'll turn around and look at him.

"Look at me," he says.

Something hot coils in my belly. It's so dark and it's so quiet, and well. I look at him.

"I didn't punch a cop."

I wait.

"I punched an MRA fuck in *proximity* to a cop. That's different."

Cool, I'm turned on again by the mental image. What is wrong with me? (Nothing; fuck those guys.) I say, to quell the nerves in my stomach, fluttering up through the pulse in my neck, "Well. You and Jaxon spend like all your free time smoking weed and that's a fact."

He's quiet for a little while, quiet enough that I wonder if maybe he's fallen asleep. Quiet enough that I find myself shifting against him, finding the perfect crook under his arm for my head to rest, cuddling into him like he's a guy I'm allowed to touch.

He speaks again, low and serious into my ear, and this time when he talks, his fingertips move against my hipbones. They are slow and non-threatening and casual, and I don't even know if he knows he's doing it except that it feels so good I'm about to full-on shudder; he's *got* to know. He says, "You sure about that?"

I intend to say yes. What I say is, "No."

His fingers freeze, just for a second. Then they begin their steady back and forth over the goosebumps on my skin again. He says, "Your cousin's my best friend and I'll have to kill you if you tell any of your people, but he gets up to some shit."

"Are you seriously telling me you've never done drugs, man?"

"Fuck no." He laughs again. "I'm saying that a full three-quarters of the stuff I've taken the blame for in your family has been Jaxon, and I've told him to let me fall on my sword because his parents know and his sister knows and I don't give a shit what everyone else thinks because none of them can disinvite me to Shabbat dinner for it."

The venom in his voice has me reeling a little.

I say, "Oh."

He says, "Like either of us has even had the damn *time* to get up to much after freshman year. We're both in core classes now, man. I'm up until three a.m. anymore, it's to *study*."

I arch my eyebrow even though he can't see it and, before I can say anything, he says, "Well. Most of the time."

"You go to Shabbat dinner?"

"Yeah," he says.

"Like . . . every Friday?" *I* don't even do Shabbat dinner every Friday. Or like. Any Friday.

"Yeah," he says. I feel him shrug against my back and ribs.

"You're not—you're not Jewish, though."

"No," he says. "Not Jewish. Just . . ." He trails off and his fingers slip under the hem of my shirt, calloused tips rubbing rough against my skin. Slow and soft pressure, like it's nothing, like *this* is nothing, and I guess it *is* nothing compared to the fact that we're basically halfway to dying on top of a mountain. But it doesn't feel like nothing.

Neither does however he was going to end that sentence.

"Just what?"

"Nothing."

"Come on."

"Jesus, don't be such a nag."

"Tell me what you were going to say."

His fingers go still on my skin and he says, "What the hell? Who are you going to tell? We're gonna become icicles up here anyway."

I swallow hard.

He says, "I'm not Jewish. And I don't really have any interest in becoming Jewish, I don't think. I just . . . god, this is so stupid; it's gonna make me sound like a kid. I'm nineteen. But—I wish sometimes? That like . . ." His voice is weirdly hoarse and I can feel his face move, like he's looking away from me even though we aren't facing each other. "That like . . . I were a Jacob. You know?"

Wow, it's like being stabbed through the ribs. I do know.

"My name even fits, right?" He laughs. If he can make a joke out of it, it won't be like he's peeling his skin away for me to inspect all his insides. "Jaxon, Jolie, and Jonah Jacob."

"You get that a lot, right?" I say.

He grunts. "I hate it."

"Yeah? Why?"

"Because I'm not one. I can't like . . . just be one."

"Why do you want to be a Jacob so bad?" I think about it—about what it means. To be a Jacob. It means being part of this messy, exhausting family that hates each other half the time, but the other half . . . well. The other half, we are moving across the entire country to be with the one who needs us right now.

I think about my zayde and the realization that if we don't get this figured out, I'll never see him again and he will just have to die without me, and it stabs me in the chest. I shut my eyes tight and force the thought away.

I can't. I can't.

I shake my head and melt back into this moment.

With Jonah.

His fingers are moving again; I'm so hyperaware of my stomach and hips—the bulge of the muscle and softness of the bump of fat and the nerves on my skin that he just. Keeps. Touching.

I wriggle farther back into him, like I can. Like this is normal.

He doesn't protest. He just widens his thighs so I can slip farther into them.

"I don't want anything to do with your parents," he says. "No offense."

That stings a little, but I very extremely get it. "None taken."

"You grandparents are pretty cool, and some of your cousins. But I don't know. Like, my family's—I'm kind of on my own a lot. They're good people, just, like, Mom's busy teaching and coaching and doing all this extra shit to pull money together because Dad got locked up when I was little for a *decade* for weed. For *weed*."

"A decade?" I sputter.

"I'm not shitting you."

Jesus Christ, *my* dad has smoked weed. And it's *legal* in Colorado. What the fuck?

"For marijuana?"

"Yes," he says, then he repeats me all primly, "For ma-ri-jua-na."

I rolls my eyes and elbow him lightly in the stomach and he closes his hand around my elbow, grinning against my cheek.

The grin fades and he says, "He's a good dad, and my mom's good, too. System wants to take Black fathers from their sons and it worked, 'cause it always works, and why do you think I want to get into politics? Why do you think activism means so much to me?"

"That . . ."

He tenses, just the slightest bit behind me, and I wonder what he expects me to say. How I'm supposed to react. There are a thousand wrong ways, I think.

I just say, "That fucking sucks."

"Yeah," he says. "Yeah. He's back now and that's good, but he works his ass off, too, trying to make up for all the years he was gone, and I just don't see much of anyone, Hallie."

I want to touch him.

I don't know how.

I just . . . stay. Right where I am. His heart beating into my back.

"Being a Jacob seems real easy from where I'm sitting. Your aunt and uncle, they're like family. They're always just—there, I guess. Adah and Reuben both treat me like I'm one of them, and you have these big family gatherings and shit, and I love that, too. I don't know. I want to be a Ramirez. I'm proud I'm a Ramirez. But I always kind of wanted to be a Jacob, too, and it sucks that I can't be."

"Yeah, you can," I say.

"Not likely."

"Family's who you choose."

He says, "Blood is thicker than water, right?"

"Pretty sure the saying is *The blood of the covenant is thicker than the water of the womb.* It's about friends becoming family, man."

"Huh," he says.

I don't even mean to say: "Not like I've ever really chosen anyone."

Jonah is a man of few words.

I say, "None of my friends even really text me anymore. I've barely moved! But like . . ." I shift against his legs and his fingers curl into my hip and I pull out my phone. "Empty."

"Well," he says helpfully, "it's dead."

I roll my eyes and shove the phone back in the bag. "It's not gonna make a difference."

"So . . ." He's kind of searching for words. Like *I can relate to this girl! Definitely! I know what questions to ask!* It comes out almost unnatural when he says, "Who's not doing the texting? You or them?" Like I asked him to braid my hair and he's fumbling.

I open my mouth to answer and then shut it again.

I don't—well, I don't know. Them.

Them?

Jesus.

I can feel the furrow deep in my brow. I want to say it's them. None of them ever really made much of an effort; I haven't had a Best Friend who wasn't just the Best Out Of All My Friends I Guess since like the fourth grade. Shelly Petryova who moved in January to Oklahoma and we never spoke again.

"I—them," I say.

Jonah drags his spine over the wood wall, repositions himself by centimeters.

"It's not like we were ever close or something, really."

He says, "Who?"

"Me and my friends."

"Like . . . all of them?"

I shrug. It physically hurts to say this, like, my stomach hurts in that same way that it hurts when a teacher calls you out in the middle of class and you're so out of it that you don't know whether the correct answer is 19 or James Joyce. "I'm busy. I'm always, I'm just pretty busy."

"Okay," he says, that quiet rasp in his throat.

"It's hard to have time for friends when you're getting a whole year of college under your belt."

"Yeah."

"Like how am I going to have time for slumber parties? I'm busy starting IVs."

"Do high school girls still call them slumber parties?"

"Sleepovers. Whatever. Fuck you."

I feel him shrug against my back. "You don't have to get defensive, dude; I'm not accusing you of something."

"Yes you are."

"What am I accusing you of?"

"Of being a shitty friend!"

The wood swallows the reverb.

I blink at the dark and breathe.

He doesn't have to say that no, he didn't say that.

And I am learning that Jonah does not say things he doesn't have to say.

Unless he's lying about the stories of the stars. But maybe he had to say all of that, too. Maybe he had to say it to keep me from coming apart.

The wind carries the snow outside, and I can hear all the little flakes tumbling, being pulled along in the dark.

Who do I even miss?

There's not even one specific name that jumps to the front of my brain; it's just *my friends. Them. Massachusetts. You know.*

I wonder if all people who have plans feel this way.

Like who the fuck has time to care about people in the kind of way that lasts past high school?

Or if it's just me.

I pull my arms across my chest, and I know it's defensive. I can feel myself trying to cover up that small piece of my heart that he doesn't get to see. I don't even really want to see it. How dare he make me look?

Who has the time or the energy? To give a shit.

I say, "We should go to sleep."

He waits a while before he says, "Okay."

And his arms tighten around me in the deep dark.

We fall asleep like that, back to chest, and sometimes I can feel the rhythm of his breathing and I know he's unconscious.

Sometimes I wake up and I didn't know I was asleep.

It's . . . it's warm enough.

But god, it's cold.

God.

It's dark.

God.

It's . . . lonely.

CHAPTER SEVENTEEN

"YOU UP?" HE WHISPERS against my neck when it's still dark outside, and I'm in that twilight state where the only honest answer is *What is it to really be awake? What is the human condition, Jonah?*

I say instead, "What is, texts you receive from an Aries at two in the morning, Alex."

"I'm a Scorpio, thank you very much."

"Oh god, even worse."

He laughs, whisper of air lighting over my skin.

"Pretty fuckin' gay of you, Jacob."

"What's gay?"

"Astrology jokes."

"Well, Ramirez, I'll have you know I'm decently fucking gay."

"Yeah?"

The wind has calmed down outside so it's dead quiet between the ask and the answer until this crying woodwind of a sound glissandos from low to high, reaching from the ground and aiming at the sky.

I tense, gritting my teeth as several others join that haunting cry outside.

They're wolves—of course they are.

And wolves can't climb trees, so the sudden fear chilling my blood is irrational. Completely irrational. But the same part of my brain that has me ducking when thunder claps or pulling my covers up to my chin when my closet door creaks open in the middle of the night has me freezing up when I hear wolves miles away on the ground.

"Yes," I say. Kind of weirdly primly, given the situation. "I've dated around the gender wheel."

"The gender wheel? That's not one I've heard."

"Honestly, it's not one I've ever said. I don't even know what it means; I'm pretty sleepy."

"So go back to sleep."

"Nah," I say, and my body chooses that moment to move, to brush neck over chest. He sucks in a breath.

He says, "I've dated around the *gender wheel* myself."

I don't know why that's surprising. I guess it's not, to be honest. Jonah Ramirez could flirt with a lamppost and get a response, and probably has. "Yeah?" I say.

"Mm. I've come to the conclusion that I'm pansexual."

I shift against him, and his stubble brushes my hair, prickles at my scalp. "What's the difference, even?"

"Well," he says, "when a man only loves *women* very much, that's what we call a straight person—"

"Ugh." I roll my eyes and shove his arm, even though the angle is difficult to hit.

I want . . . I'm looking for excuses to touch him, even though I'm already pressed against his entire body. Even though I can feel the rise and fall of his chest pressing into each bump in my spine. Rolling against every muscle in my back.

I can hear the smile in his voice when he says, "Between what? That and bisexual?"

"Yeah," I say. "Like, I'm bi. But I'm not like, only into two genders or something."

He thinks for a while.

He does that, I'm noticing. Falls into these sudden silences I never had the time to notice.

He says, "I don't know. For me, it just like . . . it fits."

That's not exactly satisfying to me, but it doesn't really need to be.

"Like," he says, "I don't know how it is for everyone else. Or for all the pansexuals in the world or whatever. But I just . . . don't give a fuck about gender. Like it doesn't even factor in."

"You don't see gender?" My mouth curls.

He sighs; it's somewhere between snarky and indulgent. "Kind of, I guess. It's like . . . I just literally don't care about it. I'm into people; that's it. Same way that I don't really give a shit about . . . I don't know. Ankles."

"Ankles?"

"Ankles," he says, and the amusement is sparking in his voice.

"Your sexual orientation is ankles."

"No, I don't *care* about ankles, Jacob. Keep up."

"Panankleual."

"Jesus Christ," he says, and he laughs into my hair.

I don't just feel it on my head. On my neck.

I feel it shooting down into my stomach, lighting up my legs, curling my toes.

I wonder if he feels the quick hitch in my breath.

If he notes it when my muscles tense.

I wonder if his pulse is pounding everywhere like mine is.

The wolves howl again and I push back into him.

His biceps tighten around me and he presses his fingers into spots on my arm that I have never in my life been so freaking aware of.

It's cold and it's scary and I can't even believe that my libido has the ability to function right now, but it *does*, and every single brain cell I have is focused on the nerves in my skin.

The spiderweb of feeling that every single movement he makes laces over me.

His thighs shift against mine.

"It's fucking cool," he says.

"What is?"

"The wolves."

I blow a breath out. Slow. Shaking.

Lean into him, because he is the only thing solid on this mountain in the dark.

"That's a constellation, too," he says.

"The wolves?"

"Mmhmm," he lies.

"Tell me about them."

"If we could see the stars right now, I'd point you to the tiniest ones in the sky. So far off you can barely see them, even now when the other ones are bright. The Greeks said that the wolves howled at night when they lost their brothers in the stars."

"No they didn't," I whisper.

"Don't be scared," he says. "They're sad. That's all."

He brushes his fingers over my arm and hesitates at my neck.

The only sound in here is our breathing in the close quiet—and the wind, which is slowly stilling outside.

The wolves.

The hairs on the back of my neck rise when I feel his mouth brush, so lightly it's almost not even real, over my neck.

The edges of his teeth.

God, I *swear* I feel them.

I curl my fingers into his thigh and release.

He breathes out, warmth at the base of my scalp.

He doesn't touch me again, not with his mouth.

I don't touch him with anything but, Christ, practically *all* of me.

The dark bleeds into morning gray.

The wolves are quiet.

CHAPTER EIGHTEEN

IT SHOULD BE WARMER when the sun rises.

Somehow, it seems colder.

Maybe because it is, and maybe because the prospect of leaving this hunting blind is absolutely fucking terrifying.

Both of us have been awake for an hour, maybe more, pretending to be asleep, because the idea of moving, the idea of descending this tree and stepping back into the snow, into the mountain feels . . . goddamn impossible.

It feels like if we stay here, huddled together, everything is okay.

It's just a night in the woods.

It's just . . . it's just a cold, poorly planned camping trip.

But the second one of us speaks, we are lost again.

We are dying in the woods.

My stomach twists in hunger, and I grit my teeth and flare my nostrils, like I can will it away. If I just sit here, muscles stiff with sleep, curled against a warm, solid boy, I won't be starving.

But it's so intense and growing until it's all I can think about. Until it feels like my stomach is gnawing away at itself.

I breathe.

Listen to the quiet.

Sink into the pain in my stomach and the sudden fear that maybe I'll be too weak to climb down out of this tree, maybe it's over now. Somewhere between last night and this morning, things have really started to *hurt*.

I am the first one to speak.

I say, "What's the plan?"

Jonah blows out a breath. "I guess . . . I guess we leave this blind."

"Is that it?"

A long pause.

"What else do you want me to say?"

I don't know.

I don't know what I want him to say.

Something.

Because I hate that the plan is wander and die.

I hate that I have *nothing* because I always have *something*, and if he doesn't have anything either then, god, we're fucked.

It's up to chance and the bounds of the human body.

And I absolutely do not trust either.

I say, quiet, just this side of a whisper, "Let's go."

Jonah takes another minute in the quiet.

Waiting.

Waiting.

Waiting.

Then we gather our things.

And we go.

The presence of those final granola bars in our bags is almost worse than if the wrappers had been empty.

I can hear it in the silence, in his voice, in mine: *Eat me. Eat me. E A T. M E.*

I shove the thought down, because if I give in now, I'll regret it later.

Then again, if I die now, I'll die on a nauseated, empty stomach, and how shitty does that sound?

I blow out a breath and shake my hands, and even that movement makes me feel weak. Like I've wasted some very essential energy.

I trudge forward, snow leaking past the ankles of my hiking boots, wrapping my feet outside the leather so they're freezing inside, even though they're mostly dry.

Neither of us talks.

We're exhausted, I think.

But also ... also, I don't know if either of us knows what to do with last night.

We've said too much; I think we can both feel it.

Like this mountain, the quiet dark and terror of survival being a question mark forced us both to tear ourselves open for one another's benefit. And now neither of us knows exactly what to do with the pieces.

The only thing to do is shut the fuck up.

I wonder if he's thinking about my inability to friend-ship, if he's wondering if I'm just an absolute, isolated freak, if he's thinking about bisexuality and pansexuality and the feeling of his teeth on my skin.

I'm thinking about all of it and very intentionally try-ing to think about *none* of it, and the distance between us is *tangible*.

He walks several paces ahead of me all day.

We're moving slowly, too slowly.

Slowly enough that it feels like we're hardly covering ground at all.

Not that covering ground matters much, does it?

We don't even know where we're going.

Toward water, hopefully, but I don't know. Neither of us knows where that water might be or if there's a river within twenty miles.

I shudder, struggling not to give into total despair, but I hate this. Being aimless.

Floating like this means . . . means things could go *any-where*. Things could be getting worse, for all I know. For us, for the people we left behind. I've been so focused on Jonah and me that I've barely even thought about them. The pangs of hunger in my stomach are swiftly joined by pangs of guilt.

I shudder again and feel my teeth begin to chatter as the white world stretches around us in dots of trees and swaths of frigid emptiness.

"You alright?" Jonah grunts.

"Yeah," I say.

We both know it's a lie.

We walk in the quiet snow as the sun rises and warms the mountain, just a little. Not so much that I'm not shivering but enough that the warmth on my face drowns out, for just a half a second, the sharp sawing of hunger in my belly.

Two degrees, difference is enough.

Enough to allow me to walk one more step, then two. Three.

God.

I'm so fucking tired.

Tears start pricking at the backs of my eyes, and the last thing I want to do is cry. Wasting water seems stupid, and showing any more vulnerability in front of this boy feels absolutely impossible.

I won't cry.

Keep it together.

Keep it the frick together.

I zone in on walking—one foot in front of the other. One step at a time. One breath, one inch, one foot. I am focused on the movement and the silence. Then I freeze.

"Jonah," I say.

He grunts. He's done nothing more eloquent than grunt all day.

"Stop."

"Listen, Hallie—I stop, I'm never moving again."

"No," I say. "*Jonah*. Do you hear that?"

"Hear what?" he says.

He stops, and I suppose this is the moment of truth as to whether he ever moves again.

"OH," he says. He swivels his head to face me, eyes wide

and hopeful for the first time since we got into this mess, and says, "Where? Where's it coming from?"

He's frantic, practically spinning in circles, because what we hear is running water.

I struggle to breathe.

I shut my eyes and listen.

"There," I say, and I just start power-walking toward the burble. It's to the west, and it's not as close as I want it to be, but it's *there*. Oh my god, it's there.

Everything in my head is screaming at me to break into a run—that the quicker we get there, the quicker, well . . . that we're there.

The quicker we can drink.

The quicker we can have a freaking *route*, a plan.

But my muscles have other ideas.

Jonah and I walk as quickly toward the sound as our bodies will allow, and when I see the stream in the distance, my legs nearly give out.

I don't even feel bad sobbing right now, vulnerability be damned.

Jonah's fucking crying, too.

When we see the sparkling bank, he does break into a run, and I'm not far behind him. It's stupid, probably, but I can't help it.

I swear, I wouldn't be capable of more excitement if a helicopter landed in front of us and offered us a ride back to paradise.

We reach the riverbank, and Jonah drops to his knees to fill his water bottle. I do the same thing, pouring the sweetest water I've ever tasted down my throat.

It's not rushing, which is nice, because, I don't know. Maybe we can like . . . catch fish or something. I don't know the way this works.

The point is it's moving, giving us a path to follow, and we're drinking.

"Be careful," says Jonah, even though I don't think *he's* really being particularly careful. "Take it slow, man, you're probably dehydrated, and—"

"Jonah," I say between mouthfuls of water.

"Hm?"

"EMT," I say.

"Right," he says. "Right."

He breathes out, nostrils flaring, and stares at his water bottle like he's physically holding himself back from downing the entire thing in a single swallow.

Suddenly the world is slow and languid, and I can feel energy seeping back into my muscles. Can feel the pangs in my belly subside enough for me to think.

Not enough, not really.

It's false.

But it's *something*.

It's . . . hope.

CHAPTER NINETEEN

WE SIT ALONG THAT riverbank for far too long—like we've reached the Promised Land, we can stop now, MAZEL TOV YOU'VE COMPLETED THE FINAL LEVEL.

As long as we stay here, we can live in that reality: the one in which we've reached the end. The one in which the final challenge is over, or, at the very least, our odds of survival have jumped by 40 percent, not by like . . . 2.

It doesn't matter.

Suddenly, when the whole world around you wants to eat you or starve you or close in on you piece by piece and you don't know if you've got two hours left or a day or a week or your whole life, things begin to feel shockingly temporary.

It feels . . . *urgent*, almost, to focus on every single thing happening to you at this very moment. Because, not to sound like a cheesy motivational speaker or something, but because suddenly, this might be it.

This might be the last drink I take, or the last time I *discover* something, or just the last afternoon I've got.

And if it is, it's important.

To just slow the hell down and languish in it.

"We should . . ." Jonah starts. He's still sitting, running his fingers over one of the few dry spots on the mountain. But he's looking up at the sky, and I'm wondering whether the sun is still on its journey up or if it's already on its way back down.

"Yeah," I say. "Yeah. We should . . ."

Neither of us wants to be the one to say it.

But I guess languishing in it, though it fits nicely with my whole newly discovered *carpe diem* thing, doesn't fit particularly well with logic. It doesn't interlace well with the goal of, you know, staying alive.

We have to keep moving.

The fact is that both of us are freaking starving, and the longer we wait to crack into the last granola bars in our bag, the slower we move.

The farther away *everything* seems.

The fact is that the longer we sit here in the cold, the stiller and cooler our blood gets, the harder it will be to get moving. The less the influence of that sudden water in our systems. The less the influence of the thrill of adrenaline at discovering the thing we've been looking for.

It would be foolish to waste the motivator of *hope*.

I am the first to stand.

Jonah looks out over the river, and I shut my eyes against the bright white and the sharp tingling in my legs and toes. I listen to the water rush.

When my eyes open, they find Jonah, hands in his pockets, standing next to me. He's staring at the water, blinking, mouth a grim line.

Jonah is a thousand miles away.

I say, "What?"

He shrugs. "Nothing."

I wait a beat. This is our dynamic, right? He's reticent and I'm chatty and I should probably just let him keep his thoughts to himself.

I say, "It's not nothing."

Jonah purses his lips and blows out a long, *long* breath through his nose. He mutters, "Jesus Christ."

"What?"

"I've been stuck away from civilization on a mountain for four days, and *still*, I can't get any peace."

I roll my eyes and shove his shoulder and his lips tick up for a heartbeat.

He says, "I don't know what I thought would happen when we found water."

I watch the river roll by.

"I guess it just seemed like . . ."

My breath clouds on the air. I say, "A finish line."

"Yeah."

We start moving.

It's a quiet walk; neither of us has much to say, or if we do, I don't think we're interested in saying it.

It's too much, the questions are too big, the stakes are too high. And it's so *stupid*, but the disappointment of finding the river this many days into this fucking nightmare and not finding a whole town attached to it is too breathtaking.

Not like that's what I actually expected to happen.

But it seems like . . . it seems like everything is vast and empty and impossible.

So we don't say much.

The glittering white landscape just spreads. And spreads and spreads, scrub brush and pine trees and aspens occasionally breaking up the white-as-a-men's-rights-meeting-in-Idaho panorama.

Jesus.

I'm getting so sick of *white*.

We crunch along in the cold, cold quiet, far enough from the river that it doesn't spray us, but close enough to keep it in our periphery. We're not risking losing it again; it may not be the key to paradise, but it's the only lifeline we have.

At least we know it's possible to get back here, if a hunter rigged a blind. That somewhere along the line, someone came out here. With gear. On purpose.

That and the water mean *something*, dammit.

It goes like that, me being quiet and contemplative, Jonah somehow managing to kind of be aggressive about it, until broad daylight shifts into evening.

The quiet, even though it's empty, even though it makes it almost impossible to focus on anything but the gnawing pain in my stomach, branching out to my limbs, my head, *god, my head*, is kind of peaceful, almost. I can begin to trick myself into thinking it's just a hike, just a cold-ass, poorly planned outing, and we'll be curled up in the bed of a truck in a couple hours. He'll have brought a thermos of cocoa and a couple blankets and we'll watch the stars and he'll try to seduce me and I'll say, "Jonah, I bet you do this for all the girls—" and be totally into it when he laughs that fucking *sexy* laugh, even when the hard ridges of the truck bed dig into my back, and—

He hisses, "Hallie."

It's barely above a whisper, but it's so sharp and sudden, and I'm so deeply, pervily lost in this *sex* fantasy, that I jump.

Am I delirious? Is this what delirium looks like? Thinking about banging in a truck bed while you slowly drift off into starving freezation? Freezing starvation. My gosh.

Jonah, I realize, has thrown his arm and is about to clothesline me if I take another step. I say, "What? What is—oh. Shit."

Just ahead of us, maybe a hundred yards up, is a moose.

A *moose*—a real, live bull with huge antlers coming out of his head and hooves the size of a Clydesdale's. And here's the thing—I don't know if you know this—but moose are goddamn *huge*. Like. GARGANTUAN.

I knew it in my head, but I didn't really *know* until this very moment, but Jesus Fucking Christ, this thing, at the shoulder, is tall enough to do dunk contests.

And he's gotta weigh, like, a ton. Not in the metaphorical way. Like literally two thousand pounds, or something approaching it. He's so huge that he doesn't look real.

I breathe, "Oh my god."

Jonah says, "They have terrible eyesight. He might not even see us. So just . . . just back away."

"I don't know, man, it looks like he sees us."

"Well, their noses are pretty killer."

"How do you know so much about moose?" I say in a tense whisper. Like that matters. Who cares.

I'm backing off step by step and he's just a couple inches

in front of me, slowly stepping back. "Scouts," he says through his teeth.

"Right. Right. Well. Should I be huge and scary? Should I—"

"No," he says, eyes on the massive creature in front of him.

The moose begins to approach us and I can feel my heart rate rise. My pulse is murderously hard and fast in my veins.

His ears pull back and I may not know moose, but it doesn't look *great* for us.

"Fuck," Jonah whispers.

"What?" I say.

"Go," he says.

"Just like—"

"Fucking *go*—run!" he says, just as the moose charges.

Oh my god.

Oh my *god*, I'm running and wishing more than anything that I had calories in my system, that I had something more than the bare minimum energy required to function right now. That my fight or flight reflex had something to build off besides pure instinct.

Walking made me want to fall; running seems like literally punching fate in the nose. Any step and I will plummet into the ground.

The bull makes a loud, horrifying noise, and JESUS I cannot be killed by a MOOSE. I can't go out like that.

FUCK.

The snow crunches over and over, and I don't know if it's my boots or Jonah's or the moose's hooves, but he's coming and he's furious and we didn't go over this! We didn't go over measures for a goddamn *moose attack.*

We're veering closer to the water, I can feeling the drop in temperature, the rise of the sound to our left. Jonah is beside me, closer to the river than I am. I move to correct our course, but the snow is a little thinner here and I can gain ground faster.

God, my muscles hurt, my lungs burn, every breath I draw in hits like a razor and I hate it, I hate it.

I hear the pounding of hooves behind me and I think, *There is no way to outrun this. There is no way. We are going to die. We survived an avalanche and days starving in the snow, and a MOOSE is going to take us out.*

The moose's hooves.

His furious snorts and sounds.

The rush of the freezing water.

And then I hear the very worst sound in the world—a splash.

It takes me a tenth of a second to see that Jonah has disappeared beside me and we're closer to the riverbank than we thought, and *god,* when did it get so dark?

"JONAH!" I scream.

It's not like the river is deep, not like it's the kind of current that can sweep you away, really, if you have any strength at all left in you—which who knows if Jonah does—it's the wet. It's the cold. It's the fact that it's absolutely *freezing* up here and getting wet means fucking *death.*

I stop to find him, and he's pulling himself up out of the water violently, like he's *furious.*

"JESUS, HALLIE, RUN," he manages, because there is

a livid wild animal running after us, but I can't leave him, I can't.

I say, "JONAH," and he struggles forward, running as fast as he can, and thank god his legs are long and he works out, *oh my god*.

I force myself not to think about the consequences for the future. About him dripping and shivering while he runs, about his *growling* and gritting his teeth and what I think might be blood on his shin. About the pallor on his face and the blue in his lips.

I think about now, this very second.

Because if this moose catches us with his antlers or his hooves or whatever the hell he wants to kill us with, we *will* die.

It's not much of a question; it's a given. Neither of us is strong enough to survive that and worry about the potential effects of Jonah being dripping wet in the cold.

The immediate concern is the seven-foot behemoth barreling toward us.

I run.

I run

And run

And run

And run.

Eventually, the thundering slows.

The terror subsides and I can see more than the barren landscape in front of me, can feel more than the adrenaline pushing through me.

I slow down, and the instant I do, my muscles rebel.

I can see the moose trotting back off to the hell from

whence he came, and for a second, I'm so freaking thrilled to have lived that I forget about Jonah's fall.

I turn toward him to say, "WE SURVIVED," and celebrate, and then I remember.

He is shaking, and yeah, he *is* bleeding—three shades paler, teeth chattering, hugging his arms around him.

"Oh god. Jonah—"

"Hallie," he says. He throws his arm out for balance, catches my gaze in his hollow one, and drops.

CHAPTER TWENTY

I AM CONVINCED THAT if I weren't totally jacked, Jonah would have frozen to death out here.

There's a little cave a couple hundred yards off, but it requires dragging his six-foot-tall ass through the snow while he freezes up, ice forming on every article of clothing on his limp body. He's completely unconscious, and I do not let myself think about the potential outcomes of that. That maybe he's a step from death and, in twenty minutes, his heart will stop beating altogether and I'll be left alone to rot (or, I guess, be perfectly preserved) up here in the Rockies.

That maybe he'll slip into a coma, and I'll have to make the executive decision to stay with his body and starve or leave and halfway murder him.

That . . . that . . .

I can't.

I can't think about that.

All I can allow myself to focus on is the cave up ahead and the burn in my exhausted, freezing muscles. All I can think about is the cave being freedom, being home, just like the river was yesterday.

If I think more than a single step ahead, I'll fucking lose it.

And we will fucking die.

So I drag him.

It's horrible outside—so cold and arid that my skin feels freeze-dried. I can barely suck the thin air into my throat. I don't want to touch my own skin; I'm afraid it will feel like paper. As soon as we get to that cave, it will all be better.

We are fifty yards from the mouth.

Twenty.

Ten.

At five, fatigue sets in, swallowing me and gashing my skin with its sharp, aching teeth.

I summon one final burst of mother-pulling-a-car-off-her-babies strength, and yank.

We're there.

Nothing sparkles, there's no WELCOME HOME mat rolled out, no end-of-the-level music that says, "Congrats! You won."

No.

The princess is in another castle.

But goddammit, we are in THIS one.

The cave isn't huge, but it's big enough; and the outside opens wide then just kind of carves back into the mountain. I don't think it exactly *tunnels* in, but it's big enough to provide some kind of shelter from the wind, the snowflakes falling from the black sky.

I leave Jonah lying by the entrance and realize how hard I'm shaking when I go for the bag. I miss the zipper once, twice, close my finger and thumb on it the third go-round.

Jonah stirs and groans and I say, "It's gonna be okay. You're gonna be okay."

There's a little indent in the rock, a shallow scoop, and the ceiling above it is black. We are not the first ones to shelter here, and we won't be the last.

Something about that is comforting. Unifying or something—which I just . . . desperately need right now. To be connected to humanity.

At this frostbitten, terrible second, I feel so utterly, wholly *alone*.

"Fuck," Jonah whispers. His teeth are chattering. "I have—I have—t-to get. These . . ." He sucks in a breath; his words are hoarse and desperate and shallow.

I slide a quick look over to him and say, "Just hold on. Hold on."

I run out of the cave and gather some nearby pine needles in my fists, scooping them in my shirt, then pour them on the ground. But . . . shit. Shit, there's no lighter, not one that's not empty.

GODDAMMIT. We're going to die out here. For no reason, we're going to freeze.

"H—Hallie. I just—"

Wait. I know this. I know how to do this! My cousins taught me, oh my god.

I yank my cellphone out of my pocket, because for some reason I'm still instinctively keeping it there, and pull out the battery. Then I shove a stick of gum in my mouth and hold the battery to the foil wrapper—rest in peace, you currently useless piece of technology.

I wait, Jonah chattering and crawling inside the cave.

I'm so focused I barely hear him.

I'm just . . . waiting.

Then it ignites.

Oh god, it ignites.

I could cry.

I think I'm kind of already crying.

I hold the little orange flame to the pine needles and they go up. YES. FUCK YES.

"HALLIE." I can hear the yell in his tone even though it's barely hissed.

"Jonah—"

"Get"—a gasp—"me out"—another sharp intake of air. He squeezes his eyes shut, lips blue. "Of these clothes."

"Oh shit. Shit I'm so sorry, I was focused on—" Even with the dim register in his eyes, I can see the flash of frustration. I cut myself off and strip his freezing, soaked shirt off his head and then his boots, his socks, his pants, his boxers. I'm in total EMT mode.

He's a patient and I'm taking care of him and he will survive this night.

He will *survive* it.

I can't even feel the cold on my own skin—not now. It's nothing. It doesn't matter.

I leave him there by the little fire and busy myself gathering kindling—aspen leaves and sticks and more pine needles and armfuls of things that will keep this going through the night.

I form a pile near the back of the cave and shove more kindling on the little fire so that it grows.

So that in a few minutes, we can actually feel warmth.

Tears sting my eyes again; I'm so relieved I can feel myself shaking.

This fire means that maybe, maybe it's okay. Maybe we are going to make it.

Maybe Jonah isn't going to freeze to death because a *rogue moose* basically shoved him into a river.

Maybe it's the comedown from all the adrenaline, maybe it's that I'm starving, maybe dehydrated, maybe the cold. And maybe it's because a rogue moose attack is just . . . fucking funny. But I start laughing.

Hysterically.

It is only when I turn to look at Jonah and see him shivering, hands around his knees, rich golden brown color back, that I realize he's naked.

My own laughter is cut off by my throat closing up.

He blows out a breath; he's not even looking at me. He's staring at the fire.

And I'm just absolutely pervily *staring* at him.

Of course I am. The adrenaline from the chase is still coursing through me at mach speed and there's this whole AFFIRM LIFE instinct pummeling my brain and *god* he's sexy as *hell* apart from all that.

Who am I kidding? Like I wouldn't take a look at the shadows playing over his musculature, the cut of his arms and the V leading down past his hips to a piece of him that rests in the dark, his arms looped around his knees . . . like I wouldn't look at that, look at *him*, under normal, regular circumstances, and feel my mouth go dry.

Like I didn't do that at the bonfire what must have been months ago but I guess was a lot less than that. Jesus, it feels like it's been an eternity. Like we never lived off this mountain. But four days ago, I wanted him up against a tree.

And now, a nightmare and a half later, I want him up against a cave wall.

I'm hungry and exhausted and cold and so calorie deprived I don't know how my brain can function beyond it. But I'm singlehandedly debunking Maslow's hierarchy of needs—all I can think is, "Touch me. Touch me. Please touch me. I'm so glad I've been brushing my teeth every day."

I clear my throat, and Jonah glances up at me as I move toward the center of the cave and carefully begin laying his clothes out by the fire.

I empty his bag. There's not much in here, not much that a fire could help anyway. An empty lighter, some gloves, which I lay out. A beanie he should probably have been wearing already. It goes with everything else. Oh hey, some spent boxes of granola and jerky (because even dying up here in the Rockies, I guess neither of us can get past the instinct not to litter?). Those, we can burn.

A baggie of weed, which I smirk at. Thankfully, it's alright. Good ol' waterproof Ziplocs.

"Hallie," he says. His voice is hoarse and quiet.

"Mmhmm." I can't look at him. God, I'm *dying* to look at him.

"Look at me."

I bite down on my tongue. I'm shaking, I guess.

I look at him.

"How you doing?"

My eyebrows hit my hairline. "How am *I* doing? How are *you* doing?" My voice squeaks, which is kind of embarrassing, but we just survived like fourteen deadly things and this absolutely stupid hot boy is naked under my blanket in front of the fire and it might be our last night on Earth and how dare he even *ask* me how I'm doing when maybe he's about to die of hypothermia?

I blow out a breath.

He laughs and says, "I'm fine."

His voice still isn't even approaching full force; it's still quiet and broken by the cold.

I say, "No you're not."

He shrugs and shudders.

"You're freezing."

"I'll be *fine*."

I blink at him. He's cold. He's approaching hypothermic.

I approach the fire and unzip my coat.

I shut my eyes. I pull off my shirt.

He doesn't say anything.

When I take off my pants, my bra, my underwear—he doesn't say anything.

I take off everything and he doesn't. Say anything.

We are the only people on this mountain and we are the only people in this cave and he is naked and I am naked and he can see *all* of me.

There's nothing else he could be looking at but the fire and the fat snowflakes blowing outside in the dark.

I say, my eyes still closed, "Body heat."

Then I can open them.

His eyes are dark and huge, like he's never seen a naked girl before, and I know he has. It's not a big deal.

It's survival.

I shiver as I slip under that blanket, wrap it around us, and press into him, each ridge of my spine pushing into the skin on his stomach. He wraps his arms around me and I can feel every shift of his muscles, the strength in his arms and in his chest and in his *jaw* pressed against my head. I shudder, and it's not because of the cool of his skin.

"Is that . . . better?" I say.

He laughs—the husky smoker's laugh I've grown accustomed to up here. "Yeah," he says. "Jesus."

I shift against him and he sucks in a breath.

I feel his fingers clench into my waist, and then they loosen.

Slowly.

One by one.

Like each release is a massive effort.

"Sorry," he says.

"Why?"

"Nothing. Sorry. Fuck."

I raise an eyebrow, not that he can see it. And shift again, shoulders slipping over his chest, god, my skin is on fire.

I'm on fire.

I can feel my heart in my throat when he exhales and it shakes against my neck.

I push back into him and it's suddenly extremely physically clear why he's sorry.

"Oh," I say. I can't help it. I laugh. I don't know if it's all that funny or if it's just a release of tension, but if it's the second, it didn't work.

My muscles are all bunched and coiled and my skin is

so hot, even in this winter cold, that I almost want to dive into the snow.

Just for a second.

If it weren't for the fact that touching this much of Jonah Ramirez's skin is fucking *delicious*, I would.

"Sorry," he says again. "I can't, uh . . . god, do you want to go back-to-back or something?"

Do I want to go back-to-back or something, Jesus *Christ* no. No I do not.

My pulse is pounding all the way in my *feet* and he's so fucking *nervous* and JONAH RAMIREZ HAS A FREAKING BONER PRESSED UP AGAINST MY ASS.

I. ME. I. Have JONAH EFFING RAMIREZ so nervous he can't think straight, so turned on his breath is hitching, and this could be *it*. This could be the end of all of it—it's that "We only have this one night!" trope that shows up every time a soldier is trying to get laid and in every third good fanfic on the internet and now I'm in it and I can't even think clearly.

How could I.

How could I possibly.

I say, "No."

He just clears his throat and whispers, "Okay."

It takes me a full minute of quiet, nothing but the cool, starry silence outside and the fire popping inside, all of his skin stealing the heat from mine under this blanket, both of us just breathing, waiting—for me to say, "This is stupid."

He says, "What's stupi—"

And I roll over and kiss him.

He sucks in a breath and doesn't kiss me back.

Until he *does*.

Until his fingers press into my back, and his other hand curls around the back of my neck and he kisses me like he's starving, like he's going to die tomorrow. He kisses me the same way I kiss him.

His teeth hit my teeth but not clumsy, not like the high school guys I've kissed. When his teeth hit mine and move to my lips, dragging across them, trapping my lower lip hard and fast enough that I gasp, it's on purpose.

It's all on purpose.

I'm on fire.

I'm electric.

Every nerve lights up like an angry sky and I drag my hands down his back.

He shifts his weight so he's on top of me and my back is on the ground. I'm acclimated to the hardness of the earth at this point, I guess, because it doesn't hurt.

"That alright?" he says, nodding to the floor.

"Yeah," I say. I could be embarrassed at the breathlessness in my voice, but his eyes light up and so why would I waste time on that?

"Cool," he says, because he's just so smooth.

It's like he hears himself say it; he briefly frowns, then rolls his eyes and shakes it off and I don't have the time to laugh because he's kissing me again, like he's practiced (I'm sure he is), like he *means* it (I . . . I really don't know how to calculate the truth of that), like it matters. Where exactly his tongue fits into my mouth, the precise slowness and strength and deliberateness every time his jaw moves when he kisses me.

I could actually *melt* from what he's doing to my mouth.

All he's doing is kissing me and I'm about to lose my freaking mind.

It's not like I've never fucked before.

I have.

But I've never fucked at the end of the world, and I've never fucked *Jonah Ramirez*, and all of these things make me feel young. So keyed up that it's like I've never touched another human.

God.

I want to ruin him.

I say, "Christ," and arch so that my stomach, my hips, my everything, brush up against him and he hisses and clamps his hand around the biceps of my right arm. He braces his weight on his hand, pressing me into the cave floor and my arm against my ribs and runs his other hand up my chest, pressure of imbalance following it where it trails.

He presses his thumb into my throat and moves to kiss me again, and I'm so turned on I can barely breathe.

I move my arm, just to test him, just to fuck him up a little, and it throws his balance off in exactly the way I intended, and he has to slip his hand from my throat to slam it on the ground, and this time when he sucks air between his teeth, it sounds a little pained.

I say, "Jonah?"

He says, "Ribs," and slides his knee between my legs to support his weight better, grabbing at his side. "I'm fine."

"Do you want to st—"

"Jesus fuck, no."

He's actually bleeding a little; I can feel it on my shin

when his leg rubs against it, and I think maybe I am, too? Because his mouth comes away from mine stained red in two small places.

But I don't care, *god,* I don't *care.*

He flips me over so I'm on top of him—very considerate, really, taking my place on the cave floor.

He says, "Body heat?" and smirks up at me.

I say, "Ramirez."

"Yeah?"

"Last night on Earth. I'm shipping off to war tomorrow. The zombies have taken the fort. The virus has spread. Soon, the nuclear radiation will leak into the bunkers. Goddammit, fuck me or regret it forever."

The look on his face—I want to frame it. He says, "*Jesus* why did I let your parents hide you?" And slips his hand between my legs, teeth on my collarbone, and I come the hell apart.

CHAPTER TWENTY-ONE

AFTER, WE LIE THERE curled up under the blanket, watching the fire. I'm trying not to think about when it will die, and that's easy to be distracted from when Jonah's fingers are running up and down my back like that, giving me goosebumps. It's easy not to think about being trapped without any food when his strong legs are pressed against mine and he's smiling against my neck.

He bites my shoulder and I yelp.

"Ass," I say, but I'm smiling. He can't see it, but I bet he can hear it.

"You like it," he says.

"Your ass?"

"Sure."

"Ugh," I say. "Conceded."

Jonah laughs and pulls me closer into him. His hands feels absolutely massive against my torso. I can't help the most private little smile. They make me feel utterly, completely small.

I don't think it's the first time I've felt this way in the last few days. But it's the first time I've really allowed myself to acknowledge it: I am not just glad to be here with another human. I am glad that the person I am here with is Jonah Ramirez.

He is not scary.

He is not a threat.

He is not this rebellious, edgy figure my parents have been wrestling me away from my whole life.

He is a boy. Just a boy. Just the boy who has forced me to rest while he built a fire, the boy who has kept me safe from wolves in a treehouse, the boy who lies to me about the stars when I'm scared, the boy who helped me survive a freaking moose attack.

He is the boy who is keeping me alive on this mountain.

I'm not foolish enough to think I'm in love with him. I've only known him, like *really known him*, for a few days.

But I know that I do love him. In a way.

Jonah Ramirez is my friend.

Like, really, *truly* my friend. In a way that almost no one I've ever known has been.

And he's absolutely stellar in the sack, which doesn't hurt as far as things to build on.

We will make it off this mountain or we will stay, but we will do it together.

As real, honest-to-goodness *friends*.

We are in this as a unit, and that matters.

I physically feel it—warmth spreading through my limbs, letting me relax into him.

Giving me five full seconds not to worry, not to be afraid.

Jonah says into my hair, "You gonna fall asleep?"

I say, "No. Aren't you? Isn't that kind of a dude thing?"

He says, "My rib hurts like a bitch."

"Sucks," I say.

He's quiet for a beat, then he says, "Wanna get high?"

I'm so surprised by that that I actually *spit* out a laugh. "Are you serious?"

"Weed survived the fall into the river, didn't it?"

"I mean, yeah—"

"So it would be a crime to waste it."

My instinct is to say, *It would be an actual crime to smoke it,* but 1) it's Colorado so it's only illegal because we're under 21, and 2) we're dying on a mountain so like . . . how illegal is it? Really.

"Not if it's, like . . . against your religion or something?"

I laugh. "Once again, not exactly how that works. Nothing in the Torah about smoking weed anyway."

I shut my eyes and pull myself away from everything else—away from the past or the future or any time other than this moment, any place other than right here.

"You know what?" I say.

"Hmm?" he hums into my back, and I get goose bumps.

"My parents were right about you. Four days and you've got me fucking around and accepting illicit drugs."

Jonah doesn't laugh so much as he cackles. "Did I hear the word *accept*?"

"Get out your weed, degenerate."

He says, "Your wish, my command." Then crawls out, still butt ass naked, from under the blanket. "FUCK, it's cold," he says.

I grin, because he's no longer in real danger, he's just, well. Naked in a snowstorm.

He grabs the baggie and rolls a joint and lights it on the fire.

Then he practically dives back under the blanket with me and throws an arm around me, pulling me into him. I laugh and shriek when he doesn't close the blanket right away, like we're kids fooling around and the air conditioner's just turned too high.

I suck the smoke into my mouth, then breathe. It doesn't hit at first, which I'm pretty sure is normal. It's been normal for me, at least. I'm high off the feeling of Jonah pressing into me and doing this illegal thing and doing it in the dark.

How the hell is doing something *forbidden* while *alone in the dark* still legitimately a thrill? After everything that's happened, after everything that's probably going to happen tomorrow, when we have to face a trip into the cold mountains without food?

I pass it to Jonah, and it goes like that for ten minutes, neither of us saying much, until the slow high really starts to kick in.

It's warm, from him, from us, from the weed. And it's quiet. I feel legitimately relaxed. For the first time since all of this happened.

Thank you, cannabis.

I stare at the fire and I'm totally mesmerized by the way it leaps, the way the little sparks jump from the flames onto the rocks without hitting either of us or igniting on the rock. But well. It's cold. It's Colorado. They're rocks—Colorado's most, as I heard, prevalent flora.

I start laughing, and Jonah says, "You good?" and that just makes me laugh harder.

Jonah peers at me, and I'm starting to look at his eyes the way I looked at the fire.

He says, "You don't smoke much, do you?"

I roll my eyes and shove him. "Yes I do. I smoke plenty."

"When?" He says it like a challenge.

"The fire! Just a few days ago! And the eleventh grade."

"That all?"

"And the ninth. Once."

His face splits into a grin and he says, "Look at you, Little Miss Rebel."

I wrinkle my nose and take the joint back from him. Now that it's really soaked into my system, I just want to keep it going. I want it to stay like this—smooth and relaxed and buzzing, kind of. Like we're the only things that are real.

"Jesus, Jonah, look at the fire."

"I know, man."

"It's gorgeous."

"It's like a painting. But you know. Hot. Burns shit up."

I sputter out a laugh. "It's like a painting but hot and burns shit up."

He gestures at the fire, all defensive. "What! It is! It's hot! It burns shit up!"

He starts laughing, too, and it's this soft, gentle thing that's so at odds with Jonah Ramirez.

Or it should be.

But somehow, it makes absolute sense to me. I feel like I know him. Better than I do, probably. But it's like I know him better than *anyone*. Better than I know anyone, better than anyone knows him. It's like we're suspended out here. In our own little world outside of everything, and nothing can touch it. We'll just exist like this forever.

"It's like you're my friend," I say.

Jonah says, "I am your friend."

"No," I say. "Not like the way people say it when they're just trying to be nice to you but then they're bullshitting you, you know? You move out of state and they don't give a fuck but they probably never really gave a fuck, and . . ." I stare at the smoke spiraling up into the black. I shake my head and blink. This is not what I was trying to say; it's not what I want to talk about with him. "Like in a different way."

His fingers start trailing up my back and down, bumping over my spine, scratching my skin. "Like a friend you fuck?"

I laugh and the dark swallows it. "Sure," I say.

Jonah's quiet. He's mostly quiet, I guess.

That's not exactly what I'm trying to communicate either, but I don't know how to phrase it or even if I should. Like if I say it too clearly, he'll think I'm confessing love to him. Like I want something more than exactly this, than exactly what we have right here, right now, and I shut my mouth.

I take another hit, and open my mouth again to say,

"A friend you fuck. Like a boyfriend. I don't know, I don't think you're like a boyfriend either."

"Not like a boyfriend," he says.

"No?" I turn over to look up at him and he pulls me closer; I didn't know we could be closer, but I guess we can.

"I don't know," he says, dragging and blowing the smoke over my head. He's looking into the depth of the cave, shadows and light playing all over his face. His jaw has stubble on it that I felt, I guess, but I never really noticed it until now. "It's like . . . it's like people think friendship and sex are these two things that only go together in romance, you know? Like it's shallow."

"I guess."

"I don't know why I'm telling you this."

"Who else would you tell?"

The dark feels vast and empty and suffocating and close all at once.

"No one," he says.

"It's the end of the world, Jonah."

He blinks, and his eyelashes are so long, and I feel a little like I'm floating. A little like I'm not tethered to anything here at all, because Jonah is floating along with me.

Then he speaks and his muscles curl and tighten around me in such a different way than they curled or tightened just a few minutes ago, and I am grounded again.

He says, not looking at me, "It's like . . . people talk about this magical thing. This thing they're always running for, falling *in love* with someone."

"Yeah. Love is a pretty normal pursuit—not a concept

I myself have heard of, but the humans do occasionally speak of it."

He grins and pulls back to shove me just a little, then pins me against him. I sigh into his chest.

"I've had best friends and I've had people I've fucked and I've fucked my best friends and I just don't think . . ." He waits. I wonder if he will ever finish the sentence. I find myself often wondering if Jonah will ever speak again. He finally says, "I don't think there's anything more for me. I don't want there to be. Like *romance* or whatever everyone, fucking *everyone* seems to want, I don't even want it. I can't tell anyone this shit because I've tried to talk about it. To a couple friends. To this girl I was seeing freshman year. To Jaxon, even. And they just always look either offended or like, *Don't worry, man, you'll find them.* And that's not what I'm trying to say; I'm not trying to say I've never been in love. I'll never find love. I'm trying to say I've found it before in people, in relationships I care so *goddamn much* about, and it never looked like wanting to slip my arms around someone and whisper in their ear while we make breakfast."

I am actually nervous to talk. Nervous to react. Nervous to do so much as make it clear that I'm *awake*, because I just want to keep listening.

"This probably doesn't even make sense," he says.

"It doesn't sound stupid."

"It's called aromantic. I guess. I don't know, it sounds even stupider to say it, like I need all these labels to define who I am when all I'm trying to do is exist. There's some ways I love people. There's some ways I don't. And it just . . . god, just because I don't want to gently forehead kiss someone and whisper that they're my world doesn't mean there aren't people I wouldn't fucking *die for*."

"It feels like we're fighting," I say on a nervous laugh.

"Sorry," he says, but he kind of *spits* it. Then I feel his breathing deepen and even, his arms tighten, then relax. "Sorry," he says again, but this time it doesn't feel like he's yelling at me. "It's just like so many people have said I'm broken or something. That I'm *not capable of love*. And that's stupid. Like fuck you, I've loved more people than any of you assholes, and I've done it better."

I laugh. "I don't think you're *incapable of love*."

"Nah? You don't think I'm a robot?"

"The thought has not crossed my mind. I can give you one of those Recaptcha tests when we get off the mountain if you really wanna prove it, though."

"I ace the shit out of them."

"We'll see, won't we?"

He sighs in my ear, exaggerated and playful, and tickle my ribs. I kick at him and his huge hands span my back.

"How about you, hmm?"

"How *about* me?"

"Love and all that shit. Give me your deepest and darkest, kid; we've only got all night."

I shut my eyes and feel the warmth of his skin, the heat on my shoulders from the fire and the bite of the wind whispering down into the blanket to touch my neck. I experience every single thing I can—his fingertips and every hair on his legs tickling over mine. Every pulse in his veins.

I say, "I've never been in love either. I don't think for the same reason."

"Have you ever said it to anyone?"

I shake my head. "Never. Not unless I mean it; I don't want to say it unless I do. How about you?"

"Oh god, yeah."

"What?" I say.

He shrugs. "I've said it so many times, it's lost all its meaning. I just figured people said it when they felt what I was feeling and then I got a little older, realized I was wrong, and whoops. Whatever. Like nineteen people are fucking welcome for my lies."

"Nineteen!"

"I'm kinda slutty, Jacob."

"I noticed."

He laughs and actually sticks his tongue out when he does. Like this smug skater cackle. And says, "Yeah you did."

"Oh my *god*," I say, and I can't believe the situation is this intensely serious and neither of us can stop laughing.

"Nineteen," I mutter. "How have you even had the time; *you're* nineteen."

He says, "One: I'm almost twenty. And two: it's easier to rack it up to nineteen when you don't date one person at a time, my friend."

If I had a mouthful of water, and god I wish I had a mouthful of water, I would have spit it out. "You just . . . cheat?"

"Swearing you to secrecy," he says.

"Who am I going to tell?"

"Say a helicopter buzzes down and rescues us tomorrow and you go back to all your Massachusetts friends or all your Colorado friends or whoever, you have to keep this to yourself."

"That you're a cheater?"

"No," he says. Sharp and clear. "That I think monogamy is for dumbfucks."

My eyebrows jump up. "So. Cheating."

"It's not cheating if everyone agrees to it."

I open my mouth to protest, but then I shut it again. I guess that's true. Nothing's cheating if you're playing by the rules. That just . . . seems . . . well. It seems against The Rules, somehow.

"See," he says, blowing out smoke. "You don't get it; no one gets it."

"You don't want to grow old with somebody? Even if it's not romantic? Like . . . what, you don't believe in soulmates?"

His big hand is firm on my shoulder when he turns me over to face him. My chest brushes his and I should be self-conscious about it but I'm not. He says, "Who actually believes in soulmates?"

I shrug. "I do."

"You think there's one person on this whole huge planet meant for you?"

"Maybe."

"What if you never meet them?"

"I don't think that's the way it works."

"What if they die of, like, scarlet fever?"

"Is my soulmate Beth from *Little Women*?"

"What if you do meet them but they're married to someone else?"

"Well—" I start.

"I'll tell you exactly what you'd do," he says. "You'd think, *I wish they were like my good friend Jonah and thought that monogamy was for dumbfucks.*"

I blink. And then bark out a laugh. I laugh so hard that I literally snort and then Jonah laughs, very obviously *at* me and my snort laugh, and I'm just laughing harder, shaking in his arms.

He whispers, "What?" against my forehead, and I say, "Jesus, I don't know."

"Do you actually believe in soulmates?"

He's not looking at me now, not really. My head is nestled into his chest and we're breathing the same air in this blanket, and I can just look right into the dark when I say it, which makes it easier to contemplate all the mysteries of the universe. "I don't know. Maybe. Maybe there's one person who's like, meant for you. But if there is, I think you have to have a chance to meet them. Otherwise it's not fair."

Jonah says, "Kids get cancer and apartment buildings catch on fire."

I say, "What?"

He says, "Shit's not fair."

I pull back to breathe, and Jonah sits up. The blanket is still around his shoulders, but we're not cocooned. I glance up at him, then up at the cave ceiling. Then outside, where the sky is dyed black and painted with stars.

I say, "Come here," and he doesn't question it; he just

scoots behind me with that blanket, and we turtle our way to the very mouth of the cave.

It's colder here, just a few feet further from the fire. But we can really, *really* see the stars.

"You ever seen a sky like that?" he says.

"No."

"I did once."

"Yeah?"

"When I was a kid. Before my dad got locked up."

I lay my head on his chest again because, well. We're naked. The cool makes it that much clearer very quickly.

"He took me out to watch a meteor shower. I remember being bummed out that it wasn't like the movies. Wasn't shooting across the sky fast, a million little comets. We went home early, but we saw a few of them. And my dad wasn't pissed I was a butt about it or anything. He made me hot chocolate. And wings. With extreme hot sauce."

He draws me in closer to him.

"How extreme?"

"Couldn't taste a thing for weeks."

"Bullshit," I laugh.

His eyes are sparkling. "Cross my heart and hope to . . . well. Anyway, he also told me about Reximus."

"Oh god," I say. "No."

"Optimus's massive pet dinosaur."

"They didn't have dinosaurs in ancient Greece."

"Sure they did."

I groan.

He says, "Otherwise how do you explain that big-ass tail?"

"Where?"

"There," he says, pointing somewhere completely indiscernible in the sky. "Right underneath Kyle."

"Kyle?"

"Yeah," he says. "Kyle, the Well-Endo—"

"No," I say. "No, no, no. I don't want to know."

He cackles into my neck and we fall into silence, looking at the spill of glitter across the sky.

I say, "Maybe there's a hundred soulmates out there for you."

He's quiet for a moment, processing. "For me, specifically?"

I roll my eyes. "Yes. The rest of us just get the one."

"See," he says, "I told you: non-monogamy is the shit."

"How's that gone for you?"

"Oh," he says, laughing, "really fucking badly. If people have been cool with it, they usually just *think* they're cool with it, and then one day they're not because they didn't actually think through everything when they agreed. People almost always think what I mean is I want to cheat, or I'm giving them an ultimatum. All I ever mean is: *hey, would you be into this idea? I'm into it and you're cool, but what if we each thought other people were also cool?* I've never dropped someone because of it." He pauses, looking thoughtful, then says, "There's been a couple. There's been a couple people I've been with who really got it. So I know it's *possible.*" He shrugs. "I can feel you judging me."

"I'm not judging you." I'm being honest when I say it.

"Whatever," he says. "We're dying; so I only have to feel this super judge ray for like twelve hours."

"Twenty-four."

"Thirty-six. Unless that moose comes back."

"That effing *moose*."

He laughs, "A *moose*. I mean, what the shit, how embarrassing."

"We get off this mountain," I say, "we're telling everyone it was a bear."

"Oh god, yeah."

"A gentleman's agreement."

I stick out my hand and he takes it and shakes.

His fingers curl around my wrist and I stare at him.

I'm sitting here with him under a blanket with my tits out and he's staring at my *face*.

For a second, I'm caught there. In the look in his eyes that I can't even begin to unravel. It's ten thousand threads of wanting and desperation and questions and fear and all the knowledge in the universe and the understanding that we are the only two humans on this whole goddamn planet.

It is not a surprise when he takes my face in his hand

When the heel of his hand, his palm, his fingers press my ear

My cheekbone

My jaw

When he pulls me toward him with the smallest pressure in the tips of his fingers and kisses me.

It is so slow that it fucking *hurts*.

I think that maybe I've never kissed anyone in my life.

We touch each other, under the black sky and a million stars that shine a million miles away, stars that make up the backdrop of this crucial twenty-four hours, this life-altering turn of a night, and that do not give a single shit about us.

We are not imprinted in the memory of the stars.

Anyway, it's the vastness of the black that's imprinted in mine.

We shift back into the cave, inch by inch, toward the warmth of the crackling fire.

Eventually, we pull apart.

Jonah adds a few sticks to the fire and I shift back against him.

He starts to run his fingers over my hair.

I breathe out a sigh, the smallest, most inexplicable smile touching my mouth.

His hand carelessly brushes across strands of my hair, and we're both breathing in smoke and I think, absently, that I bet I'll go out smelling like a campfire, and then the thought drifts off on the wind.

It doesn't matter.

Tomorrow doesn't matter; all my ideas and plans for after and speculations and . . . they don't matter.

This matters.

Feeling every single bit, every single pinprick of sensation in my brain and blood and skin right here right now is the only thing that matters.

Ever.

I feel.

Every single bit.

Every single pinprick.

When he sucks in the shallowest breath.

Then he releases it and his arm curls over my torso and

he brushes his fingers back and forth over the softness of my stomach.

I should not feel safe.

But I do.

He says into my ear, "Jesus. I'm snuggling you and I'm totally into it. And not even in a horny way."

My own laughter is the thing that lulls me into sleep.

CHAPTER TWENTY-TWO

THE SECOND THING I notice when I wake up is the storm gathering outside the cave. The sky is growling, and rain is pouring down.

The first is Jonah shaking me and yelling, "Hallie. HALLIE," in my ear until I nearly haul off and punch him in his beautiful, perfect face.

"Oh my god," I groan. It's still dark outside, for Christ's sake. And my limbs kind of hurt. One in particular; I must have injured it yesterday—surprise, surprise.

I'm cold.

I'm hot.

I'm annoyed.

He says, "Hallie, someone's here."

That wakes me up.

I jump out of the blanket, then realize I'm naked and it's freezing and quickly burrow under it again, yelling at Jonah to grab my clothes.

Even under the circumstances, he smirks.

I blush.

Then I start yelling again.

He tosses me everything I discarded last night in a fit of hypothermic passion, and I say, "What makes you think there's someone here? Not some*thing*, right? Not like another killer moose or wandering bear or—"

"No," he says, holding out his hand and staring outside. "It's someone. I swear, I heard—I think I—it sounded like . . ."

I hug my coat around my shoulders and grab his hand, then tighten my fingers. "Sounded like who, Jonah?"

"Like—like your cousin. Like Tzipporah."

"*What?*" I say.

Hope chokes me. I shove it down and grit my teeth. It can't be her; it can't be them. That's just—it's too much to want. It's not possible.

He's hallucinating, maybe.

Maybe he's just that far gone, and this is it for us.

I shut my eyes tight and brace for the possibility.

I feel Jonah's fingers crushing over mine and he tugs me closer.

"Hallie?" he says.

I open them.

"Do you trust me?"

I blow out a breath. It slides out onto the ice air in a white cloud. "Y-yes," I say.

We leave the cave together.

It's a full minute of walking, and then I see it: a bobbing flashlight.

"Oh my god," I breathe. "Oh my *god*."

My exhausted legs do not leave me the choice of running—I can't do anything more than walk, but I'm crying. This is it; this is it.

It's someone.

We get closer to the light, and I hear what Jonah heard: "HALLIE."

I sob. *Immediately.*

"We're here!" I scream back, but my voice is swallowed by thunder.

The crash is so massive I can *feel* it in the ground. Lightning makes the whole sky electric white. I jump.

I would shrink back against Jonah in service of some kind of evolutionary BIG GUY IS PROTECT kind of instinct, but he jumps harder than I do, so I just keep walking, shouting out that we're here, we're here, WE'RE HERE.

The snowmelt seeps into my jeans, leaks into my fire-dried boots, but it doesn't matter anymore, does it? We're found. We're saved.

We're *okay.*

I shout again, ignoring the persistent crashes of thunder, the ever-brightening sky, the sharp, freezing rain now pouring from the sky.

I don't hear Tzipporah's voice first; I hear Jolie's.

I can't run to her, but she's running to me.

The thunder and lightning are nearly on top of one another now—one massive cascade of sound and light— and I ignore it, it barely even registers, until Jonah screams, "FUCK," and a tree just yards ahead of us cracks and bursts into flame.

He shoves an arm out on instinct and I run right into it, screaming, because the tree groans, sparking and smoking and blazing, and every one of us hears the *s-p-l-i-t.*

The sky, and the fire before it's drenched by the rain,

are kind enough to illuminate the entire scene as it plays out: the dramatic *Homeward Bound* limping toward each other breath before the reunion—and the branch of the old, dry, dying tree cracking off and slamming into my favorite cousin.

Suddenly, I am more than capable of running.

I sprint off toward her, gritting my teeth past the pain in my leg from whatever irrelevant thing I did to it yesterday, and make it to her just as three of my other cousins catch up.

I do not have time to ask where the others are.

To ask why only the older ones are here.

To contemplate all the horrible reasons it might be that the only ones I see are Tzipporah, Sam, Jaxon, and Jolie.

I only have time to *fix things*.

I snap out, "Where? Where did it hit her?" and Tzipporah swings the flashlight to face Jolie, who's gasping for breath.

The massive branch has her thigh pinned to the snow.

"Jolie?" I say, "are you bleeding?"

"I don't—I don't know, I don't know, I just—"

I say, "We have to get her inside," and stare at Jonah, who immediately rushes to her side and starts looking for a handhold. "Christ, Hal," he says, eyeing me over the branch. "It's heavy. I can't—"

"Lucky I've got these massive guns," I say, and I pull, but he's right. I can't possibly lift it.

"I don't know how we're supposed to do this," I say.

"You don't, dumbasses. There's five of us." The other three situate themselves around Jolie. She coughs out a sob.

Right. Right, it's not just us.

God. It's not just us.

I have to laser in not to cry from the unbelievable relief.

We count.

And we all lift as a unit.

It's heavy and dense and the tree groans when we pull, but we *do*, and Jolie scrambles out from under it.

"We have a cave," I manage, and as the sky absolutely drenches us and spurs us on with its furious crashes and streaks of lightning cracking in the air, we run.

Jolie props herself up between Jaxon and Sam, and they do most of the work pulling her along.

Finally, finally, the mouth of the cave appears, and we all settle in.

Jaxon gets Jolie in one of those thin heat-holding blankets paramedics give people in all the movies (they're life-saving little things), and I do a check to make sure she doesn't have anything worse going on other than some cuts and major bruising. Then Jaxon takes out a lighter and reignites the fire with that and a fire starter kit he also has in his Mary Poppins bag of holding.

Tzipporah, meanwhile, has handed everyone bottled waters and granola bars, and I meet Jonah's eyes when I dig into mine; I don't know which tastes better: the water or the food.

"How the hell have you all fared so much better than we have? Well. Wait. Wait, where are Lydia and Oliver? Oh my god, are they dead? Oh my god."

"Hallie," says Jaxon, and he clamps his hands around my shoulders. "Hallie. Hold on."

"Are they okay?" Tears prick at my eyes and I'm shaking and I'm hot all over. I'm so *hot* suddenly.

"They're *fine*," he says.

I blink.

Sam says, "We were found a day and a half after you left."

"Oh," I say. "Oh, thank G-d." I'm relieved for them. And I'm furious. This was all for nothing—why are we so *stupid*.

"We tried to find you. They all did—Search and Rescue, everything," says Jaxon. "But you—" He looks up at Jonah and something passes between them. Something intimate and brotherly and desperate. "—you were just. Fucking *gone*."

"How?" I whisper.

"Hunter's field cam," says Sam. "You tripped it with motion. A hunter caught onto it being weird footage and turned it in. We came up here to find you, but Search and Rescue said no. There was apparently some sort of 'big storm' coming or WHATEVER."

We all laugh, too hard, too loud, a release of a million kinds of tension.

"So you just . . . you just came up here? Without them?"

"You're family," says Jaxon, and I . . . I start to cry.

Despite the fire, I'm absolutely freezing, so I lean back into Jonah and let my eyes shut lazily, open slowly. I'm so suddenly safe. Relaxed.

The storm is wicked outside and we'll be here another night, but we are *family*.

And we are okay.

Jonah wraps his arm around me and brushes my hair back from my forehead—a combination of gestures that raises a few eyebrows but no one says anything.

Then he says, "Jesus, you're hot."

I suck in a breath and move to respond with something cute or snarky, but suddenly my teeth are chattering too hard.

"You're clammy."

"It's the rain."

He draws his hand back and tightens it around my arm to turn me to face him.

"Hallie, are you okay?"

"Yeah," I say. It comes out a little breathier than I intended, but I'm sure I'm fine. I'm sure it's nothing. I'm just weak because of this whole shocking ordeal. Because of surprise and relief. Because . . . I'm still hungry. Dehydrated.

I say, "I'm fine," and the breath catches in my lungs. I feel hot and cold and my leg is so hot, it's so hot, and it *hurts*.

I'm so weak?

When the hell did this happen?

I was fine last night, and I was fine pulling Jolie to safety and sitting here talking and now . . .

The adrenaline of everything is beginning to wear off and things are starting to *hurt*.

I reach for my leg and pull back like it's on fire.

Jaxon furrows a brow. "Are you—is everything okay?"

"I don't—" I move to unbutton my pants and say, "Turn around. Don't look; it's weird."

Jaxon throws his hands in the air and spins.

I yank my jeans down around my ankles and almost scream when the fabric slides over my shin.

"JESUS CHRIST," I yell and Jonah curses.

"Don't look," he says, but it's too late.

I've looked.

My shin is swollen. It's bright pink and shiny red and furious. "Oh my god," I say.

"It's fine." He says it like he's desperate.

"Jonah."

"It's fine; put your pants back on."

"I can't," I say.

"Yes you *can*—you're going to freeze, Hallie."

He's using my first name and that scares me, or it would scare me under normal circumstances. It should scare me, a lot of things should, but I just feel like I want to crawl into my bed and never come out.

My leg is infected.

That's the long and short of it.

My leg is infected up here on a mountain and I can't even put my pants on over it and I'm still starving and still dehydrated and we're trapped by a storm and this is it.

This is what does me in, I guess.

Jonah goes searching for something in his bag.

"*Shit*," Tzipporah breathes.

I love it when Tzipporah swears, under typical circumstances. Not right now. Right now it scares the hell out of me.

"Jonah—" I say, and Jonah emerges from his bag with a pocket knife.

Adrenaline kicks me into awareness. "What. What is that."

"It's infected," he says.

"Yes." I can feel my pulse pounding in my ears.

The sweat drying on me and the pain on my skin and

the infection in my leg that popped up overnight. Who even knows when I got it? It could have been *anything* that did it. Big or small. I bet it was running from that big, stupid moose.

"I think—okay listen, don't look at me like I'm completely nuts, but I think if we try to relieve the pressure . . ."

"Absolutely not," I say.

The thought of anything touching my leg after the jeans about made me leap out of my skin makes me want to die.

"You can't cut her *open*," Jolie says, and I can hear her voice shaking with my entire body.

Jaxon says, "Jonah . . ."

Jonah ignores everyone but me. "Hallie—"

"No," I say. "No, you can't. We can't."

"You can't walk on that."

"Yes I can," I say. I roll over to my butt and move to stand, and the pain in my leg is astounding.

My breath leaves my body.

I crumple.

"You can't even put on pants. Hallie, I don't want to do this, but we've got to give it a chance to drain."

"I can't walk or touch my leg with fabric," I say through tears pricking my eyes, "and you think our best option is to slice it open?"

He throws his hands in the air. Then he says, "Yes!"

I stare down at my leg. At the livid, swollen flesh. At the knife glinting in Jonah's hand. And back at my shin. "I don't . . . I don't want you to do that."

The water crashes down outside. I swear it's like living

in an air bubble under floodwaters. My absolute horror is punctuated with the thunder.

"How far away is your truck?" I ask, biting down on tears.

Tzipporah says, "A couple miles."

"I can make that," I say, and move to stand again, but when I do, I collapse again. The sudden drop in energy, the exertion of the tree on Jolie—everything is coming to a head.

"You can't," says Tzipporah. "None of us can. Those roads are absolute mud now. And we can't go out in that." She looks down at my shin. "Jesus, Hal."

"What am I supposed to do?" Jonah says. Then, "You're the EMT. You tell me." His shoulders drop and the relief on his face is palpable. It's not on him anymore; it's on me.

And everyone has stopped objecting.

Which means I have to be the one to decide that he needs to slice me open.

I stare down at my leg. It's pulsing now, pain pumping through it and fading and spiking again. "Fuck," I whisper. It comes out with tone, and I squeeze my eyes shut. "Yeah, you're going to have to do it. Just. Cut me."

Jonah sucks on his teeth and the knife starts to shake in his hands. "Yeah," he says. "Okay."

I blow out a breath. I'm shaking. I don't know if it's because it hurts or because I'm cold or because I'm scared.

I almost feel like it's pointless. Like, who gives a shit; we're going to die anyway. But I'm also not so committed to death that I can give up because my leg hurts.

I grit my teeth.

"Do you—" Jolie starts. "Do you need my help? Do you

want me to—" She cuts herself off. She's still trembling from the pain of her leg, and who honestly knows *what* damage sustained—and she sees it, I know. The intimacy between Jonah and me. The new intangible thing that says, *I trust this boy more than anyone I've ever known.*

Of course he'd be the one to do it.

Why would anyone else?

Jonah closes his hand over my thigh, each finger pressing into my skin. "Don't move, okay?"

I'm trying not to cry. "Okay," I say. It's hoarse.

He breathes. Steadies the knife.

"Sterilize it!"

He jumps. "Fuck. Right. Right."

Both of us release a wave of tension, like Jonah needing to take a moment to clean his knife means that by the time he's done, everything will be better. Like the delay will mean he doesn't have to cut my freaking leg open.

Jesus.

He hands it to one of my cousins. I don't even see who; I don't care. They come back with a knife that's dripping with rainwater and hand it back to Jonah.

I shudder.

I hug the blanket around me like safety.

"Hallie," Jonah says.

I shut my eyes and clench my jaw.

"Hallie."

"What?"

His hand is on my shin, clamping down, holding me still.

"Look at me."

I do what he says.

He stares at me, and I can feel the cool of the blade on my leg.

I gasp from the gentle contact, but he doesn't look away. He holds me there in his solid gaze. I can't look away and I don't want to.

We are the only ones in this cave. It is only us. Just him and me.

Nothing else exists.

I can feel my breath speed, my pulse spike.

My fingers rub threads of the blanket and I just—I don't think. I give him the tiniest, non-committal nod.

And he cuts.

I fucking *scream*.

"GOD," I yell, and my back arches and I curl down over my stomach, hugging my leg to me. I'm sobbing, it hurts so intensely and coldly and *Jesus* I can't breathe.

Jonah grabs my leg and straightens it and wipes away the infection with a small piece of cloth Jaxon hands him. He applies a little pressure and I choke on how badly it hurts, on the crying. It's getting the infection out as much as it can, it's necessary it's necessary it's—

"Okay," he says. "Okay, Hal, sshhh."

He grabs me by the shoulders and pulls me into him, pressing me into his chest while I cry. Eventually, the throbbing dies down and I can't feel blood and whatever else running down my leg, and that's what Jonah says, "We need to sterilize the wound."

I mumble into his chest, "I didn't bring a first aid kit because I'm stupid."

He says, "No shit."

I furrow my brow where he can't see and he backpedals. He says, "Not that you're stupid. That you didn't bring a first aid kit."

"Mmm, likely story."

I shiver again.

Now that the immediate terror of the leg slice has worn off, I can feel the wreck that my body has become again. I burrow deeper into his chest, like he can fix it.

That's when he says, "Listen, we can't just let that sit there wide open."

I shrug. I'm so tired.

He says, "I don't know what else to do."

"Excuse me," says someone.

I think Jonah is done speaking so I open my mouth to say something exhausted and he continues, "Urine is sterile. It works as a disinfectant."

"What?" I say into the fabric of his shirt. It comes out, *Whhbbb.*

"EXCUSE ME," says someone.

I hear the telltale *thwwppp* of a zipper and I say, "JONAH!"

I recoil and he says, "WHAT. What else am I SUPPOSED to do?"

I say, "WELL DON'T JUST FREAK OUT AND PEE ON ME!"

He blusters.

"PINE SAP," I say. "Pine sap oh my god."

Jonah raises an eyebrow.

"You're the Boy Scout; you should know this. Put your dick away."

"My dick isn't out, Jesus Chr—"

"Pine sap functions as a disinfectant."

"Oh," he say. "Oh, thank god."

"You sure? You weren't set on *peeing on me*?"

"No," he says. "That's white people shit."

I choke and laugh. Then choke again on the pain. "It's antiseptic. And anti-inflammatory. And it legit closes wounds up; seriously, what did they teach you in wilderness survival?"

"EXCUSE. ME."

We both blink.

Sam throws her hands in the air. "Not trying to kink shame here, but of course we brought first aid? You absolute idiots?"

"Oh," I say. "Oh. Oh right."

I don't know how I keep literally forgetting they're here. They're here, they came into the mountains to rescue us, but it's like I don't know how to rely on *anyone* but myself anymore.

As though I was ever great at that in the first place.

But they feel fake, like hallucinations. I keep instinctively falling back on us being completely alone.

"So not. Not pine sap then," I say.

Sam says, "Or piss."

I laugh, and for a second, I forget how much everything hurts.

Then my breathing slows and Jonah's smirk disappears.

I stretch when Sam pulls out a first aid kit—antiseptic, bandages, whatever else. I stare up at the smoke-stained cave ceiling while she works on me, focus on the divots and changes in color and texture in the stone.

If I think about that, I can think past the searing pain in my leg and the worry in my chest that I'm so hot even in this cold. That I'm shivery and weak and am having a hard time thinking clearly.

That I'm so desperately avoiding looking at my leg because I do not want to see those telltale red lines traveling up from the wounds.

I hate that I know, in my silent heart of hearts, that what I am showing are signs of sepsis.

When Sam pours something over my leg, I start giggling.

"Hallie?" It's Jaxon. Haha.

"It kickles." I frown. "Kickles."

I feel Jonah's hand on my back.

"*Tickles*," I say, then I burst into harder laughter.

"Hal?" says Jonah.

"Mmmhmm?" The world starts to swim, just a little.

Jonah does a double take, staring down at my shin. "You're—oh. Oh shit."

I shut my eyes tight and force them to blink open. "What?"

"How are you feeling?"

"A little weird. Cold. Ha."

"Hallie," he says, and he grabs my shoulders and runs his thumb over my shoulder blade. "Focus, yeah? How do you feel?"

I shake my head. "I'm okay. I'm just kind of hot and sweaty. And tired; I think I'm just tired."

He purses his lips and his gaze tracks from my eyes down to my leg. "Don't freak out."

"Lines?" I say.

He swallows. "It's going to be fine."

"Mmm."

"Listen to me, Jacob. You're—we're. We're going to be fine."

I say, "Okay," and I shiver and shake through slipping my jeans back on.

The cousins are all quiet.

No one says anything all night.

Jonah lets me stay under this blanket with him near the dead ashes of the fire and fall asleep.

CHAPTER TWENTY-THREE

I SLEEP FITFULLY.

I shouldn't be asleep.

I should be moving.

But everything hurts.

I'm hungry and I'm thirsty, and by *hungry*, I mean my stomach is twisting in on itself.

By *thirsty*, I mean my mouth is so dry I can barely swallow. I mean it's literally painful to open it to talk. I mean my lips are dry and cracking and I cannot believe that I am drenched in sweat.

How much more.

Can I possibly sweat.

I drain a water bottle and still, I'm freaking dying.

I'm fresh out of energy and I can't stop shuddering and I think it's the shuddering that keeps waking me up.

Sometimes I wake to Jonah holding me so tight that I can't really shake, and I think I've fallen still. I think I am warm because of him and that the worst has passed.

But then I can feel his heart beat against my back and I

should be getting warmer; his body heat, even through his clothes, should be helping. But I'm so cold.

Then I'm on fire again.

I can't even think right to remember what's a good sign and what's bad.

My jaw hurts from clenching my teeth and I'm so.

Tired.

Snow begins to fall in place of last night's rain storm and I don't know if it started when I was sleeping or if I was staring out at the great white nothing and just . . . failed to notice it.

Sharp flakes fall from the deep gray and I say, "We should move."

Jonah says, "What?"

Sam says, "*What?*"

I say, "We should—we should walk. We should go. We should . . . we should . . . the truck . . . we . . ."

He moves very close to me, and I can see that his eyes are laced with violent red.

"Are you okay?" I say.

"Am *I* okay? Jesus, Hallie."

"I like it when you call me Jacob," I hear myself say, and I curl up against him and drift into darkness.

The next time I'm conscious, I don't know how long it's been. The sky is still that milky gray, and the snow is falling, but it's doing so with purpose. With fury. There were hours of peace in the early morning between the thunder and the snow, but the temperature has dropped by degrees and the world outside doesn't look peaceful anymore.

It looks scary.

I can't feel the fear, not really. Not as deeply as I should, I don't think.

But the sky looks violent.

I hear shuffling deep in the cave. Then something smacks against the cave wall and I hear a loud stream of swears.

"Jonah?"

SWEAR SWEAR SWEAR SWEARING SWEARER SWEARING SWEAR.

"I can't—FUCK, I'm sorry; it's this wind. I can't get a fire going; are you cold? Are you cold, Jacob?"

There's a flurry of activity—multiple cousins moving at once and everyone freaking out and—

"We have to get her out of here."

"She can't stay any longer; I don't care if it's snowing. We have to get to the truck. Someone's gotta contact Search and Rescue."

"Jolie has to stay."

Jonah's voice: "Jolie can stay with her. I'm fast; let me and Jaxon go—"

"Stay," I say. "Jonah." I've never done this before in my life. Needed someone enough to beg them to stay with me.

I say it again: "Stay."

Jonah moves so fast; one second he's far away cursing at the darkness and the other he has my face in his hands.

There is nothing complex about the way he looks at me.

Jonah Ramirez is afraid.

The wind kicks up.

Sam, Tzipporah, and Jaxon leave.

They've been gone for a few minutes as a new storm—or the colder, more wicked piece of the last one—builds outside.

Then it breaks.

The whole entire sky is a dam and it releases with fury.

Jonah is shaking and I can feel myself slip.

I can feel it all just . . . slip away. Breath by breath.

The snow is a wall outside. But—

It's not the cold of everything around us that gets to me in these last five minutes—it's the heat building in me.

The way my mind races hot and fast, knowing there's no way out of this cave.

The warmth that spreads through my body against the furious wind outside, the rock and ice walls of this cave—warmth that feels a whole lot like those last hazy seconds before sleep.

The smoke and red in Jonah Ramirez's eyes when he grabs my jaw and says through clenched teeth, "Don't. Hallie Jacob, if you give up on me now, if you leave me alone up here, I will *never fucking forgive you.*"

I blink.

Slow.

Breathe.

One Mississippi.

Snow and wind beating against the trees, the ground, everything, everything.

Two Mississippi.

Lightning, flash against a tree, snap and crackle and the clean stench of burning wood. They call it thundersnow, not that that matters now.

Three.

Three.

I breathe the cold into my lungs.

It all feels like ice. But touch it long enough, and ice starts to feel like fire.

I brush my hand over Jonah's knuckles on my jaw.

The world lights up like a flare.

CHAPTER TWENTY-FOUR

I HAVE SECONDS TO feel it
before the world goes gray

Two more
Three
and

CHAPTER TWENTY-FIVE

I WANT TO TELL everyone to stop touching me, stop touching me, my skin hurts, everything hurts.

I'm so thirsty.

I'm on fire.

Stop touching me, stop talking to me.

I try to talk but I can't. I'm just being *jostled* everywhere and how am I supposed to focus through this?

I say, "No no," and that's about all I can manage.

There are hands on my torso and my legs and people are being so loud.

So loud.

I think: *Where is Jonah?*

I think: *I will never fucking forgive you*

I think: *STOP TOUCHING ME*

I stop thinking.

When I do wake up, for real, it is to fluorescents and an IV in my arm.

There is a persistent beeping beside me and there are thin sheets over me and I feel like I can breathe.

I blink up at the ceiling, at the sterile flicker of the lights, and close my eyes again, listening to the shuffle of feet and the murmured conversations and . . . and what that means is that I am in a hospital.

I am . . . I am off the mountain.

And I am in a hospital.

Oh my god.

Oh my *god*.

My heart rate spikes and quick fear clutches at my chest. "Where's Jonah?" I say.

There's a gasp at my bedside, and my mother falls on top of me.

She's hugging me so hard and she's crying, sobbing in a way I've never seen her do.

"Hallie?" My dad's voice is low and strained. He's never been less than totally composed and controlled, but when he says my name, I hear only the raw.

He lets out one monstrous sob and catches it, then kneels by my bedside, his head touching the edge of the bed, touching my side.

"Oh my god," he says.

And then I'm crying because it's over. It's over and I'm alive and it is remarkable how quickly it all starts to feel like a dream.

I wait. I wait for what feels like forever but what is probably not more than sixty seconds, then I say: "Where is Jonah?"

My dad tenses just the slightest bit beside me; it's instinct, I guess. A tiny piece of me is mad, but I just don't have the room in my body for that feeling. I don't have the energy.

My mom says, "Jonah's okay."

I nod and clench my jaw.

And then I cry.

My cousins come visit me, too. Everyone does. I haven't gotten to see Jonah yet, but it's okay; I guess it's okay. Because I am dying to see everyone else. They saved us. They risked their lives to save us. Because we are *family*. Of course, we were complete morons for leaving like that, but Jaxon is so quiet and gentle about all of it, like I'll break.

Now that we are out of crisis, everyone can release their emotions in a flood.

Jolie vacillates between desperately relieved, crying and hugging me, and furious. She's not worried about the storm and her leg and our lives and now, so she's just letting everything go.

She's so mad that she had to process me dying.

That they all had to deal with the likelihood that we were gone forever.

I get it.

I get it.

But we weep into each other's shoulders at the end of everything because she saved us. They saved us. Despite everything. We're okay.

It's all normal.

It feels . . . normal?

It all feels . . . wrong.

It feels good to wake up in a bed, to be hydrated, to get shitty hospital food that tastes like it was made by a Michelin-starred chef.

To have my family again.

It feels *good*.

It also just feels . . . off. Strange. Maybe to be separated from Jonah by people and walls and wires and normalcy.

It feels off and I feel so far removed from all of it—almost numb. Like it never happened, like it isn't real, but also like it's the only real thing that's ever happened in my life, and this has got to be what's fake. Hasn't it?

I think about these things when I am granted a few moments of quiet.

When I am alone, I consider the depth of apathy about everything and the deep dark of the mountain sky and the questions of what the hell happened to me. For minutes at a time.

I am not disappointed to be off the mountain. I am breathlessly relieved.

But I also know that I have no idea how to be here.

I have no idea how to talk and function normally and wake up and brush my teeth and order food and . . . I have no idea.

I have *no idea* what comes next.

CHAPTER TWENTY-SIX

WEEKS PASS.

They pass strangely; compared to the few days on the mountain, everything moves too quickly. Twenty-four hours feel like twelve. Ten. At first, everything moves on fast forward. There are too many voices and too many visitors and too much talk about what happened to me.

But then it's like it stops altogether.

Everyone begins to slide back into normalcy. We take turns sitting with Zayde and bringing food to him and staying the night. I start classes at school and everyone has heard about what happened over break to the new girl, but no one knows me, and so every time someone asks me if it's okay, it doesn't feel like concern; it feels like voyeurism.

No one slows down to rubberneck when they pass a big accident on the highway because they're concerned. They do it because they're curious.

I hang out with Jolie, mostly, and she and the arts crowd protect me from assholes dying for a little drama that can't affect them.

It's normal, anyway.

I'm back to the daily grind.

And so is everyone else.

Little by little, hour by hour, we all start to forget.

At first, my parents were extra attentive, coming into my room to check on me all the time, going out of their way to bring me stuff, even being super cool with Uncle Reuben and all of them.

But now, well. Well, it's been a couple weeks and no one is afraid that I'm going to disappear in the snow, a body to be found years later, frozen at seventeen in the headlines.

I sit at the kitchen table, scrolling through my phone, and find myself on Jonah's Instagram. He hardly ever updates it so I'm just mindlessly thumbing through the same old stuff I do every morning.

Every evening.

The pattern, I guess, is comforting.

Or something.

I don't know, but I know that when my mom says, "No phones at the table, Hallie," the urge to snap at her is instant and overwhelming.

I clench my teeth.

But I put my phone away.

Mom says, "How was school?"

I normally just let it slide at *Fine* because I don't want to go into shit with them. I don't want to go into it at all, and I honestly don't know if it's because now I'm super depressed or if it's because I always felt like this.

This is how it is now, since the mountain.

Everything feels *wrong*, and I am eight thousand percent uncertain.

I fucking—I fucking *hate* uncertainty.

God, I've never been *uncertain* in my life.

And now here I am, unable to remember what my policy on school details has always been, and when my mom says, "Did you want broccoli or carrots or both?" I reply, "I don't know."

I don't know!

I don't know anything anymore!

I blink hard, enough that my eyes start to sting. I mean to say, *Fine*. Like always. But what I say is, "I'm a goddamn spectacle, Mom."

My mom says, "Language."

My dad sets his knife down with purpose and says, "Hallie Jacob."

I blink.

I pick up the fork.

I eat my broccoli and carrots I could not choose between, and I am absolutely suffocated by the fact that I seem to have changed utterly while my parents simply have not.

Nothing else has.

Nothing but me.

The only one who notices, or notices and cares enough to bring it up, is Zayde.

He and I have never been close; we never really had the opportunity to be. But I love him and he loves me and he's known me all my life.

It's my night to hang out with him, and we've been playing pinochle in the quiet. He doesn't have much to say nowadays; I think it just takes a lot of energy.

But he lays down a jack, wrinkled hands trembling, and says, "Buttercup. You've looked better."

I wrinkle my nose. My pajamas are mismatched, and I guess I could have taken more time on my hair but—

"Sad," he continues. "You look sad."

"Oh," is all I can manage.

He doesn't push me. He just takes a card from the pile and pushes his glasses up on his nose. And he waits.

I finally say, "I don't know why I'm being like this. I should be happy. I survived."

"Not enough," he says, glancing up at me and resting his elbows on the table, "just to survive."

I blink back at my grandfather, and for a second, I feel sorry for taking up the most precious of all his time—the time that comes near the very end—with neediness. With sadness. With my own drama.

But then he gives me the smallest smile and goes back to his hand, and I think he'll make a run.

And I don't feel sorry at all.

Jolie and Jaxon invite me over for Shabbat dinner.

I say to my parents, "I'm heading over to Uncle Reuben's."

My mom waves me off and my dad says, "Let me drive you."

I don't know why that's so irritating, but lately, everything is irritating? Which is stupid because I survived! I survived a week on a mountain in the cold with a boy I didn't even know! I should have a new lease on life! I should be clicking my heels together and diving into paintings to play with all the animated woodland creatures and sing songs about joy.

It's fine.

I'm just completely empty, is all.

Because no one gets it.

No one but Jonah Ramirez, and he hasn't texted me and I haven't texted him, and I think neither of us knows what the hell to even say.

The car ride is weirdly quiet.

It's not enough, I hear. *Just to survive.*

I shut my eyes.

We get to my cousins' house, and Dad comes to the door with me and says hello to his brother; they were so cool for a while—everyone was. Like this almost-tragedy really brought the family together.

It seemed, through family dinner after family dinner, that maybe the change was going to be permanent.

I don't know, maybe it will be.

I slip in the front door and Jaxon whacks me on the back of the head affectionately. Jolie beams at me and says, "Lila Rahal asked me to Winterfest. Like as her date. Oh my god, LILA RAHAL. Do you even understand how beautiful she is? I think she's going to wear a suit. Kill me now so my heart doesn't literally stop when the most gorgeous freaking girl in the school shows up at my DOOR in a SUIT; you and I are going dress shopping. Oh shit, I need to figure out what color hijab she's going to wear so I can like, coordinate."

"Lila Rahal, Jesus—well done."

Jolie is not lying; Lila can absolutely get it.

"I thought—weren't you into Yvette?"

"No," she says. "Hallie, pay attention. That was weeks ago; Yvette's with Angel."

"Oh," I say. *Pay attention. Pay. Attention.*

My cousin wrinkles her nose, smiles, practically starts doing pirouettes.

See now, *this*. This is what I should be doing. I should be experiencing this kind of glee at every flower and shooting star I see.

I smile at Jolie.

I hope it looks real.

Here's the shitty thing: I'm happy for her. It's not like I've been through this life-changing thing and now her date with the prettiest girl in school is just so trivial that I don't care about it.

It's that I don't care about . . . anything.

Because I don't know how to care here.

I don't know how to care when the world has stayed the same and I'm just totally different and probably traumatized, and what I really do not know is how to navigate all of this without a plan.

Anyway, I smile wide and bright.

Jolie accepts it.

I wait to hear the front door close and for Uncle Reuben to come back in and for Aunt Adah to light the Shabbat candles.

But what I hear, what we all hear, is Reuben hissing, "You have got to be kidding me," and my dad saying, "Jesus, Reuben, why does everything I say have to be insulting to you?"

"I could ask you the same question."

"Are we seriously doing this again?"

"You're the one coming into my house shitting all over it, man."

I don't know why hearing things like *Man* coming from adults is strange, but there's something to be said for the weirdness of parents reverting to their teenagehood when they're yelling at each other.

The whisper-yelling lowers and then it's quiet because my cousins and me are shamelessly eavesdropping.

"Thought they were done with this shit," said Jolie.

"Please," says Jaxon, "they're never done with this shit."

I'm quiet for a minute. Then I say, "No one's done with this shit because nothing's changed. Nothing changes."

Neither of them knows what to say about this.

So it's quiet and now it's awkward with *them*. They know I'm talking about the time on the mountain and we've all been pretending it's the same for everyone. That it bonds all of us. I want it to! In some way, it does. None of us will ever untangle what we did for each other on that mountain.

But it's not the same.

They were stuck for two days.

I thought I was going to die.

And I spilled my most intimate secrets to a boy I didn't know and we haven't spoken since and it feels like an absolute chasm, jumping from me to anyone else here.

Dad and Reuben are still fighting, and the silence between me and my cousins is suddenly palpable, and all of this is so *trivial* and *shitty* and *stupid*.

Dad says, "HAL," and I say, "Fine," before I even know what he's going to say.

He's done this before—no surprise he'd do it again.

When I'm eighteen, I'll do what I want.

But at seventeen, I still have to listen when Dad yanks me out of my cousins' house because he and his brother can't seem to stop hating each other.

I fling my overnight bag across my shoulder and stomp out of the house, and I don't even say goodbye to my cousins because I'm a bitch.

Well, that and who am I kidding? I left without a fight because every single place I go, I feel alone.

And with them, with my *favorites*, I feel even lonelier.

Because they are my people.

And they were up there on that mountain.

And they don't get it.

I press the heels of my hands into my eyes and sit in the front seat while Dad mumbles some sort of half-hearted apology that's really just apologizing for Reuben's terrible behavior, when let's be real—it's not really about Reuben. It was always about my dad and everyone's too afraid of him to say anything about it.

I keep my mouth shut while he guns for approval and continue to dig my hands hard enough into my eyeballs that I see those weird tie dye spots that don't go away for five minutes even after your open your eyes, and finally, when we near the house and Dad is *still* talking, saying more to me than he has in the entire two weeks I've been home, I just . . . snap.

I snap.

I say, "Dad. I'm sorry. Why don't you just fuck off?"

He jerks the car into park in the driveway. "Excuse me?"

"You've been the worst to Reuben our entire lives because he smoked too much weed growing up and you think he freeloads or whatever and you're so much better and we're so much better because we have money and he's so *irresponsible* and *wild* and has to ask his parents for money sometimes—"

His nostrils are flaring and I think he's angry, but more than that, he's hurt. He looks *desperate* when he says, "You have no *goddamn* clue what you're talking about; you weren't there twenty years ago or five years ago when—"

"I don't *care*," I say. "CHRIST. Does anyone get it? That I just don't—" I choke on a sob. "I don't CARE."

I jump out of the car and slam the door behind me and my dad says, "Young lady, you can't speak to me that way."

He's trying for authority, but he feels betrayed that I would take his brother's side over his. I can hear it.

It just feels so *wrong* and *stupid* and *wasteful,* I guess.

I stomp off to my dad yelling and chasing after me and I don't care. I'll care tomorrow probably when I'm grounded within an inch of my life, but right now, I'm in the kind of mood that gets a girl to tell her dad to fuck off and slam the door when she gets upstairs and just keep the door locked while he pounds on it.

I wait until he goes away.

I pull out my phone and scroll through Jonah's Instagram again and again like that will get me some kind of connection to him, and then I close the app with fervor.

I feel so goddamn empty.

And alone.

And grateful to be alive.

Alone.

I blow out a breath.

I scroll to Jonah's number in my phone, a number I was never supposed to have but got once when I was fourteen and never deleted in case it stayed his number.

And well, just on the off chance, I write *Hey.*

CHAPTER TWENTY-SEVEN

JONAH WRITES BACK AT 2:00 a.m.

He says: *Hey stranger*

I say: *wyd*

I understand that that's code for *Do you want to fuck?* But I don't care. Maybe I do. Maybe I do want to fuck, maybe I want to talk, maybe I want to go back up to that cave where I felt close to anyone and anything and had plans for the next five minutes, because the next five minutes were all that mattered.

Where life wasn't so wide open and impossible to organize.

He says: *Nothing. Wanna smoke?*

I don't know if I want to smoke.

Like I said, maybe.

I say: *Where can I meet you*

He shoots off an address that's about halfway between his side of town and mine—both considerate and sensible; maybe this is where he and Jaxon go to hang and be degenerate.

I don't worry too much about being quiet when I leave

the house. Mom and Dad go to bed at like 11:00, and I'm sure they're deep into REM cycles by now.

I don't slam the door or anything.

But at this point, even if they heard me leave, what's the worst that happens?

I shrug to myself and hop in my dad's car.

I drive off.

It's so quiet at night on the roads. There's no snow around, which is nice, no ice to worry about, which hardly ever happens around here in January, but small blessings. It is empty, just this wide, black stretch of road ahead of me, the occasional flash of headlights through the windshield.

I get to the address Jonah gave me, and it's not a building; it's a trail.

It's thirteen freaking degrees outside but somehow that seems right.

It seems right that if we are meeting, it's out here in the cold.

In the skeleton shadows of the trees.

I slip out of the car and lean against the hood, hugging my huge coat around me.

It's not the one I brought to the mountain; that one is buried in the back of my closet because I couldn't decide if I wanted to keep it forever or burn the thing.

It's big and warm, though, and marigold yellow.

I'm surveying the dark trees ahead of us while my nose goes red and cold, lost in a thousand quiet things, when the quiet rumble of a truck engine makes me jump.

Jonah pulls up beside me, Rage Against the Machine blasting through the doors.

He turns off the ignition and opens the door and the music quiets and it's back to the sounds of the woods—which is to say, almost nothing.

The woods in Colorado are quiet, always. Almost eerily so.

But there are a couple crickets. An owl somewhere. Breeze rustling the twiggy fingers of the leaflorn aspens.

It's quiet, still, when Jonah gets out.

He takes a couple steps over to me, hands shoved deep into his jeans.

"Aren't you cold?" I say, nodding to his hoodie.

He shrugs. Then he tips his head toward the trail and I follow him to the entrance.

"It's closed," I say, but even as I vocalize it, I know it's not a real protest.

"So?" he says.

He hops the thigh-high closed gate, totally ignoring the sign that lets hikers know that it's closed after sundown, and I hop it after him.

After . . . everything, I guess he's right. Trespassing on a little walking trail in the middle of the night is nothing.

He walks ahead of me, and I'm struggling just a little to keep up with his huge, long legs. My muscles are burning a couple minutes in, because this is apparently the most physical activity I've engaged in since the mountain.

Which honestly feels like it should be bolded and capitalized or something at this point.

Like . . . The Flood. The Shot Heard 'Round the World. The War to End All Wars.

THE MOUNTAIN™
Hallie Jacob (PTSD Pictures, Coming to a Theater Near You)

Anyway, my muscles hurt, and my lungs feel a little overworked, a little dry, like they did here before everything happened.

I'm glad I'm far enough behind Jonah that he probably doesn't notice.

Well, kind of. Except that ostensibly, the reason we showed up here wasn't exactly to hike; it was to . . . to what?

I don't know.

Wow, I guess I really have no idea.

Maybe he doesn't know either or maybe he does, but if he does, he ought to share it with the class, because god, I'm *drowning*.

I half-jog to catch up with him, and then we're walking in step, even though I'm burning my muscles harder to do it. I refuse to fall behind again.

"Why did you come out tonight?" I finally say.

Jonah stops and whirls on me. "Why did you ask me to?"

I fall back just a half step, just a shift of my weight onto my back foot, and I blink.

"I don't know," I say.

He stares at me, eyes dark and intense and glinting deep, black-brown in the moonlight.

His jaw is clenched like he's mad, almost.

Or like . . . something hurts.

I can't even tell the difference anymore; maybe there isn't one.

He doesn't look away, doesn't shift backward, just looms there inches away from me, hands still in his pockets.

Waiting.

Breathing.

Each time either of us exhales, it clouds out on the clear dark.

I feel like there's something I'm supposed to say or do but I don't—I don't know what.

Welcome to my freaking life.

My pulse is jumping, faster and faster the longer he looks at me, cool in my cheeks warming as I wonder.

Then he just makes this sound between his teeth, and his hand is cupping the back of my head and yanking me toward him.

We knock teeth and my nose bumps hard into his and I don't care; I don't give a *fuck*.

Jonah's hands are on me, and his tongue is playing in my mouth like desperation.

For a couple of seconds, I can just lose myself.

I can kiss him and touch him and be touched over this jacket, under, until I forget that I'm so fucking alone.

We both can.

It's freezing and dark because this is how it is with us; this is how we connected, so it's fitting that this is where we wind up, kissing each other like we are both hungry.

His teeth catch my bottom lip, and I think one of them is a little chipped because when I run my tongue over my lip, it's raw and tastes like blood, but I don't care, I don't care.

I care that, for this second, all there is is me and Jonah and a hundred trees that have no opinion, a solid dark that surrounds us, that lets us both just *exist* in a way that is shockingly alive. Shockingly . . . connected. Like, Jesus, I forgot what it felt like not to be numb, not to be isolated.

Right here, right now, I'm not.

He pulls away from me after who knows how long, fingers curled around the back of my neck, pressing my forehead into his.

I feel the warmth of his breath on my mouth, on my nose.

I keep my eyes shut against all of it. I don't want to talk or think or see; I just . . . want to feel.

He is the one who speaks first: "I don't know what the fuck I'm doing, Jacob."

I open my eyes and pull back. I want to say something; I try to. But then suddenly I'm crying. I'm just . . . crying.

Sobbing.

Like, feel it like a knife in your gut, cannot do anything to quell the total onslaught of pain *weeping*.

I actually curl in on myself—grab at my stomach crying so that my hair falls in a tangled sheet around my face.

Like I need something to hold onto and it might as well be my own skin.

Jonah steps into me and wraps his arms around me, tight, so I'm bound there against him. So I can fall the hell apart without actually shredding at the seams.

He holds me together.

And when I stop crying hard enough to hear him, I can tell that he's sniffing and not in an *it's cold* way. In an *I'm fucked up, I'm crying, too* kind of way.

It doesn't make me feel lonely or fragile or like I don't have something to hold onto.

It makes me feel like I'm not alone.

For once.

It makes me *feel*.

"Jesus," he says when he finally pulls far enough away to really look at me, "have you just been a total fucking wreck?"

"YES," I say, and now I kind of want to laugh. Like everything has been muted for weeks and a thousand things want to burst out of me at once.

I do start laughing, and Jonah runs his hand over my curls. His mouth turns up and he says, "You spend a week up on a mountain and suddenly it's like *drama* happened or something."

"Tell me about it. Like *please, it's not as though everything in your entire psyche is different now and you're fundamentally altered! Get it together!*"

"Honestly. Fuckin' embarrassing."

I laugh a little more, but it's more like a release of breath, a release of tension.

Somewhere in the 150 hours we spent up there, that became normal. And everything back here became wrong.

But with Jonah, in the cold, in the dark woods, I can feel again. I can *experience*.

He sits, right there on the cold ground in the middle of the trail, pine needles crunching under his butt.

I sink down with him.

"It's weird, right?" I say.

He doesn't have to ask me what. He just says, "Yeah."

"I don't know how to talk to anyone."

"I can barely hold a conversation with Jaxon. With *Jaxon*."

I throw my hands in the air. "What is wrong with us?"

"First guess would be a lot."

I smirk. "Don't forget; I know all your secrets. It's not a guess."

He throws his head back and laughs, and when he looks back at me, it's like he's surprised by it.

"I don't . . ." I say. "I don't even know if I want to be a firefighter anymore, Jonah. Like, what the hell? How can one thing like this just change *everything*? Like my whole . . . my whole personality. I can't plan anything; I don't know what I want or how to get it even if I did, and it's like everything is a huge question mark now."

He shrugs. "Probably PTSD or some shit. I don't know, we're probably depressed."

"Probably."

"Therapy would be good, maybe."

I repeat, "Probably."

He's quiet.

I say, "Sounds kind of exhausting, though."

"God, *right*?"

"I missed you," I say.

"I didn't think I missed anyone," he says. That stings a little. But then he says, "I can barely feel anything, man. Except then you texted me and it was like . . . well. I was wrong. I missed the hell out of you."

My face brightens; I can feel it. "You did?"

"You're my friend," he says. "Like . . . not in the way that Jaxon's my friend. Or Jolie. Or my quad mates back at school. Or . . . or like anyone else is. It's different."

"Different how?"

"Different like we *shouldn't* be friends, really. It doesn't make sense. But you know shit about me that other people don't and we almost fucking died together and you . . . you *get* it."

"I get it," I whisper.

His knees are touching mine.

Part of me wants to ask when class starts back up for him.

But the other part doesn't care. Like why does that matter? Why does that matter when we are in the woods together *now*?

"You're still gonna fight fires, Jacob."

The easy confidence with which he says it, the familiar use of my last name, the pressure of his knee on mine, give me butterflies.

"You think?"

"We're gonna get therapy and/or brain drugs and/or whatever and do what we have to do and we're gonna get everything figured out."

I dig in the earth just a little, so my fingertips are blacked with dirt, itching with dry pine needles. "I don't know if that's true."

"Well," he says, "me neither."

I burst out in laughter.

"Could be total bullshit," he adds.

"Oh thanks for that, that helps."

He stares at me, smile in his eyes.

Because, well, it does.

Maybe it helps for someone else to be unsure.

My whole life, it's been map this and that and lay out a chart and navigate this way and this plus this equals the desired outcome, and my whole life in front of me.

But what matters to me now, in this moment, is the sharp question mark of it all.

The vast unknowing.

Jonah leans a little closer to me and says, "I am kind of cold, now that you mention it."

"I mentioned it like twenty minutes ago."

"I don't care."

I say, "Well, what do you want me to do about it?"

He shrugs. "I dunno. I kind of like it."

I slide so that now his knee pushes into my thigh. He glances down at it.

It is incredible how a person can be so utterly relaxed and so on alert all at the same time.

My muscles are uncoiled, my mind is not racing but it's not numb, it's *right*. But I can feel every single movement Jonah Ramirez makes, down to the little lightest shift when he *breathes*.

We are shivering here, talking truths in woods we shouldn't be in, and it feels right.

Suddenly, I am afraid.

I am afraid that everything feels right, right here, right now, and the second we get in our cars to leave, all the wrongness will return.

I will feel like some kind of alien creature who doesn't know how to exist in her family, with her friends, in a convenience store, on the highway, on the freaking Earth.

And after this, this thorough hour of *belonging*, that seems intolerable.

I quell the train of thought with, "How's everything with your family?"

Jonah glances up at the sky. It's painted with stars. Not in the same way it was on THE MOUNTAIN™, but it glitters enough to draw the eye. He says, "Back to normal."

"Same," I say.

"It's weird as hell," he says.

I wait.

"Like everyone else is the same and that's so . . . fucking impossible. Because how can that be when you're so . . . so goddamn *different*? Right?"

"Yes. Yes."

He draws in a breath and stares at the ground, the trees again, the stars again.

It is full minutes of silence before he says, "We're gonna have to get out of here eventually."

I say, "Yeah."

I do not want to.

I want to stay.

It is two more minutes before he says, "It's cold."

I shut my eyes and draw in a deep breath. And I stand.

Jonah stands with me, and this time we walk together.

I don't have to run to keep up with him; we step side by side, shoulders brushing, path criss-crossing just a little, in the way that no one really walks a straight line.

Eventually, the trail entry shows itself, and I jump the gate first.

Jonah follows just behind me and walks to his truck.

He stops.

Like there's something he wants to say, and I'm hoping he does because . . . it feels like—it feels like if we drive off now, he'll go to school and I'll go home and that will be that.

This will be something we had and he will be someone I had and it will all be past tense, and we'll just . . . move on.

Until I see him sometimes at Jaxon's.

It feels like a crossroads.

Like he will always be Jaxon's.

Or he could be mine, too.

I don't know why *I* can't make myself say anything.

Jonah twirls his keys over his finger, catches the cold metal. He glances down at his own hand and twirls them again. Opens his mouth.

Shuts it.

Opens it again.

His hand is on the handle to his door.

I feel it in my chest. The thread between us, tensing, stretching, one more second and it will snap.

I say, without a story, "Did I ever tell you about the constellation Stormpilot?"

His mouth twitches up. He looks down at those keys, at the handle.

He finally says, "You hungry, Jacob?"

I look back at the woods and bite my lip. "Starving."

"Tell me about it at breakfast."

He smiles, big and genuine, and I jump in his truck.

We don't say much to each other in the closeness of the vehicle, just listen to Tom Morello rage for a while and watch the street signs pass.

There's a little twenty-four-hour diner just up Colfax, and I'm certain that's where he's going. That's somewhere our lives have intersected, I guess, though we knew nothing about it.

He pulls in and parks, and we both take a little too long getting out of the car.

There's a couple people in the diner besides us.

It feels strange and right all at once.

It's warm in here, and brightly lit, and smells like cinnamon and okay eggs and decent coffee—like a twenty-four-hour diner on the middle of Colfax.

The waitress brings us coffee without either of us asking.

Jonah opens a menu, and so do I, and I settle into the softness of the seat across from him.

My foots brushes his calf and he doesn't pull back.

The waitress asks our order.

I want cinnamon rolls. He wants steak and eggs, which I am certain will be pretty shitty—who orders steak at a diner?

It is so . . . regular.

I don't tell him about Stormpilot.

Jonah clears his throat and sips his coffee and says, "This is kind of shitty, huh?"

I laugh. "Yeah, it sucks." And I take a huge drink.

He looks sleepy and disheveled and comfortable, and like everyone looks under fluorescents.

He grins at me.

I eat my incredible cinnamon roll and he starts on his mediocre steak, and at first it's so quiet that all we can do is listen to the other diners' conversations.

But somewhere between bites, one of us has started talking about school.

About EMT work.

About that movie that could be the best thing to have ever been written or the literal worst.

Somewhere between 3:00 and 4:00 a.m., our stomachs are full and I have shed my coat and he keeps kicking me under the table.

I light up at the touch.

I laugh when he says something stupid, and he laughs when the waitress spills water on me.

I drink another shitty cup of coffee.

I am alive.

The End.

ACKNOWLEDGMENTS

A stormy book for a somewhat stormy time in my life. Thank you so much to those who helped me weather it, in a million different ways. First, my agent, Steven Salpeter. You are, as always, a force of encouragement and belief and indispensable advice on tea. (Two tea bags for Irish breakfast! What a revelation.) Holly Frederick and Maddie Tavis, I could not ask for two lovelier humans to have in my corner. Thanks so much for going above and beyond for me and my wild little books. To my editor, Nicole Frail, you are an absolute delight to work with. I am so grateful to have the chance to tell stories with you. To Nicole Mele and the rest of the amazing team at Skyhorse, thanks so much for every single thing you do to make my years-long dream of becoming an author a continuing reality.

Thank you to Colleen Oakes for constantly being a wonderful writing friend and providing support and critique and the warmest friendship from three thousand miles away. To Rae Loverde, Slytherin badass love, wonderful friend for the texts that cross like ships in the night, and for everything you did and always do to help me and my words. You are indispensable.

TO YOU, gentle and punk rock reader. Here's to you. A toast of whatever beverage you're into. Thanks for everything. Everything.

And last, not least, family. Humans with whom I cohabitate. Blur, thanks for the phrase "that's white people shit." Boys, Mal and E, you are what makes everything worth it. And Sara, well. Critique partner, co-writer, fave, actual not in any way related family: *nose wrinkle* You invited me into your home on PURPOSE; you did this to YOURSELF.

ABOUT THE AUTHOR

Photo by Taylor Whitrock

BRIANNA R. SHRUM has been writing since she could scrawl letters. She digs all things bookish, geeky, superhero-y, gamer-y, magical, and strange. You can usually find her writing under her Harry Potter tree, and drinking chai (which she holds as proof of magic in the world). She is also the author of *Kissing Ezra Holtz (And Other Things I Did for Science)*, *How to Make Out*, *The Art of French Kissing*, and *Never Never*. She lives in a Charlotte suburb in South Carolina, with her favorite people.

MORE FROM BRIANNA R. SHRUM AND SKY PONY PRESS